Freyja's Garden

MARY DOCKRAY-MILLER

SIGNUM PRESS

ISBN (paperback): 978-1-959360-12-4
ISBN (ebook): 978-1-959360-13-1

The cover image is from a photograph taken by Mary Dockray-Miller of a section of Edwin Austin Abbey's mural *The Quest and Achievement of the Holy Grail* at the Boston Public Library.

Contents

Ne huru Hildeburh   herian þorfte
Eotena treowe;   unsynnum wearð
beloren leofum   æt þam lindplegan,
bearnum ond broðrum;   hie on gebyrd hruron,
gare wunde;   þæt wæs geomuru ides!
(*Beowulf* ll.1071-75)

Chapter One

The women climbed slowly to the crest of the hill. One by one they reached the top and stood breathing fast, nodding to each other as they scanned the ocean from the plateau.

The bay spread beneath them, blue and tranquil as the sun began its rise over the land of the Scyldings. It was a harbor to be proud of, with coves and inlets for protection from storms and enemies, rocks covered with delicious mussels, schools of fish, and beaches big enough for boat building. The chill and the salt air made Hildeburh remember last autumn, after her father had returned, and the boats were repaired. She had sat on a huge, sodden log, stirring the tar in a kettle to keep it pourable; Hnaef and the other boys used bundles of twigs to slap the tar on the boat sides and then flat wooden scrapers to smooth the edges so the boats would cut, watertight, through the

grey waves. Her father stalked among the boats and the
workers and warriors, supervising, helping, teaching. She
remembered, when he had stopped to admire Caedmon's
handiwork, how the iron circlet around his neck had
gleamed with its ambers and amethysts from summer
raids. Caedmon the bard was also a carver, and he was
replacing the front of Hunlaf's ship. The old walrus
had been knocked into the sea by a catapulted rock,
and Caedmon was creating another, fiercer and larger
than before. Others fixed shattered oarlocks and replaced
benches, mended sails and reinforced storage boxes. Boat
season was brief, between final harvest and the first snows,
but crucial.

The men had left the day before in those same boats,
Hoc's dragon boat leading the fleet from winter harbor.
Now in the early spring morning, the ten-year-old girls at
the end of the line shivered in the wind. Their bare feet
looked bluish white on the rough grass of the hilltop, and
their short wool smocks did little to dispel the chill. Their
breath came quick with excitement, and it hung in the
clear air like a light mist.

The women formed a horseshoe-shaped ring with the
girls in the center, the ring open to the sea and the sky,
sun rising onto their backs. Almost all the Danish women
were here, Brigga enormous with her third child and Ahla
humpbacked with age. Even the wasting sickness could
not keep Anya from the ceremony; Hildeburh looked at

Anya's over-bright cheeks and her thin arms and recalled that Freawaru had said that Anya could not live through another winter.

As the sun became fully visible over the water, old Bruna began the chant. Hildeburh stood with the other girls. Sunya, her playmate, grabbed her hand as the two of them watched the sun's ascent and listened to the chant that made them women in the eyes of Freyja, the mother goddess. Bruna's words were from an ancient ritual that had existed since before anyone could remember, before any of the battles the bards sang had happened, before the death of the white christ god that Hengest talked about endlessly after the last viking raid.

The language of Bruna's chant was so old that Hildeburh did not fully understand it, but she caught some of the words before the wind whipped them over the headland away from the sea: ocean...Freyja...then the goddess' name again, then something about daughters and gifts and the earth. Hildeburh rubbed her free hand against her smock, trying to warm it.

Last night, the hall had seemed empty after the spring departure of the men. Hildeburh already understood that all men left every year; she had taken great pleasure in teasing Hnaef that he was not yet old enough to go on viking expeditions. Hnaef had cried. Later, when Hoc, her father, said goodbye to her and told her to look after her little brother, she felt a new responsibility for Hnaef and was sorry she had made him cry. Hoc's beard had tickled her cheek when he kissed her. She missed him already, but when Bruna had gathered the girls together, after the washing and sweeping were done, and had told them what would happen the next morning, the pain of his absence receded.

"Freyja is the greatest of all the gods. She is the giver of life, older than any of the other gods. The men say that she is merely Odin's wife, that he is the All-Father, with the wisdom of Yggdrasil, the World Tree, but women know this is not so. You are old enough, now, to be women and to know that long ago, Freyja was the queen of all the gods, and there was no king. Every year she took a consort and gave birth anew to the grain and the fruit, and every year the consort died after he received the most exquisite pleasure of union with the goddess, mother of all." Hildeburh had always liked the stories that included Freyja, the wife of Odin, but had never thought of her as having any special powers of her own.

"Then the darkness fell on the northern lands, and the raiders from the west came and killed the cattle and burned the crops. Some of them stayed; others were driven away. But war has a price, and the war gods gained power, and the goddess who gave life but not victory was neglected. Soon Scyld Scefing came, and worshiped Odin, and conquered the lands of the Danes, and the worship of the goddess was not neglected but forbidden, for Scyld had no use for any gods but Odin and Fenrir.

"But even men must be born, and even warriors must eat, and the forces of the goddess Freyja are strong yet. The babies are born, the cattle are raised, the harvest is rich; Freyja still favors us. We women keep her worship strong, and we know her power and fear her displeasure. She is loving but terrible, giving but stern. Men have little to do with these life forces, and they see Freyja merely as a wifely companion to Odin rather than as a powerful goddess."

Hildeburh felt the slight ache on her forearm where she and the other girls had made shallow cuts and sworn on their blood to keep the rituals and wisdom of Freyja secret, never to reveal it to the men. Sunya had been the one brave enough to ask what Hildeburh was thinking. "If Freyja is so powerful, why keep her worship a secret from the men?"

Bruna had smiled and given Sunya a necklace made out of wooden beads. Its pendant was a statuette of Freyja, sitting cross legged on her big bottom, her large breasts and shoulders under a face serene if not beautiful. "I make one of these, every year, for the girl brave enough to ask," she said, and Hildeburh looked with envy at the necklace and wished she had spoken up.

"The men are not here in the spring and summer, Freyja's most powerful time of birth and fruit." Hildeburh thought about that, and for the first time realized that most babies were born when the men were away. One summer old Oslaf had stayed home with a broken leg and had gone to live in the sheep shed on Black Mountain, returning only when all the babies had been born. Bad luck to have men around at baby time, Hildeburh remembered the women saying as Oslaf had packed a bag of provisions. When a baby did come in the winter, it usually died. Freawaru said Anya was a winter baby. She had always been frail.

Bruna's voice called Hildeburh back to attention. "...and since the men are home in the winter, filling the hall, hunting and fishing, the earth and its fruit are sleeping. Freyja sleeps, and we take care of our men and our homes and wait for the spring, for birth, for fresh grains, and her worship. It is Freyja who attends us when we bleed." Hildeburh and Sunya smiled at each other. They had both begun monthly bleeding this past winter and often searched together for the special moss that grew under the snow, tucking it into their wraps to absorb the blood.

"Freyja is there when we bring children into life, with pain and blood. She is there when we tend the dying. She has no interest in fighting, in weapons, in raids and in ships. When the men come home, and speak of these things, Freyja retreats from our world."

Bruna spoke of a time soon after the great king Scyld, who named the tribe of the Danes after himself long before Hoc was king, when the Scylding men fought among themselves, and the Jutes had come from the north, burned the hall and the long houses, killed many men, and taken the women back to Jutland as slaves. Like it or not, women needed men to protect them from other men, even as Freyja disdained such a world of killing and raiding.

Sometimes, Bruna said, Freyja did require a daughter during the spring ceremony, and a girl would be swept by the wind off the headland and into the sea; that had not happened since the time of Bruna's great-aunt, who was Freyja's priestess when Beow was king and the Scyldings controlled the inner sea. Freyja had always had a priestess among the Danish women, Bruna said, although the men tended to think of her more as a healer than as a priestess.

Still clutching Sunya's hand, Hildeburh watched as the women broke into groups. Bruna and Ahla started a fire and placed an iron cauldron on a flat stone among the burning twigs and branches. While Ahla filled the kettle with water from a skin bag, Bruna moved among the groups of women, muttering and handing out small amounts of something; Hildeburh couldn't see what it was. Hildeburh's mind started to wander; she shivered and thought about how she'd like to be back in Hoc's hall in her bed of woven cloth with the fur sewn on it. Soon, she and Sunya and the others would start sleeping outside, away from the musty confines of Hoc's hall and the burum. They would roam the hills, tending to sheep and making sure the ponies didn't wander too far.

The men had taken many of the ponies—short, stocky animals with long coats and tangled manes—with them on their viking expedition. Hildeburh had heard, in the songs that Caedmon sang after the feasts on cold winter nights, that warriors mounted the ponies and then charged into battle, gleaming like flashes from Thor's hammer, Mjollnir, scattering the enemy and returning with wealth, plundered supplies of cloth, armor, weapons.

Last winter, Sunya had told Hildeburh that she didn't believe all the stories Caedmon sang. Hildeburh had been shocked at the time, but then realized that Sunya was right. If all of Hoc's conquests were easy and splendid, why did so many men come back with terrible wounds, and some not come back at all? And sometimes ponies didn't return either. Hildeburh never asked, but she suspected that they were eaten by the warriors or killed in battle. That was why every spring the men left most of the mares in Scyldingland with a few of the stallions—to ensure they would always have enough ponies.

Maybe Sunya and I will be pony girls this summer, Hildeburh thought, and not have to work in the gardens like last summer. She remembered that Hnaef had already asked to take care of the ponies when the chant of the women changed, bringing Hildeburh back to the headland, warmer now with the sun fully over the horizon. Bruna, Ahla, and a few other of the older women started a new chant, which formed a background for the songs of the remainder of the ceremony.

All of the women with children, including Hildeburh's mother in her purple robe and golden braids, gathered around the kettle. The slave women who were mothers stood as well; Bruna had told them the previous night that the goddess honored all women, all mothers, both free and enslaved. Hoc brought slaves, women and men, to Scyldingland at the end of every summer; prisoners from his raids were ransomed back to their tribes or taken as part of the plunder. Some were sold or given away; others stayed to serve the tribe, clean the hall and the outbuildings, do the cooking, tend the fields. Female slaves were expected to provide sexual services for the men. Those for whom these unions had borne fruit had equal place at the cauldron with the Danish mothers. They sang:

> *Grant us daughters, grant us sons*
> *Grant us wisdom, grant us strength*
> *and take our children*
> *and take our selves*
> *We birth in blood*
> *We die in blood*

As the women threw things into the boiling water, Bruna stopped her chant and whispered to the girls about the special powers of mothers who had known the pain and pleasure of giving birth. "You, too, if the goddess blesses your haemod with a baby, will know the ultimate exultation that comes with the pain of bringing life into the world. It is the highest honor to Freyja and from Freyja."

Next, the women in the group who were not mothers made their contribution to the boiling water. Hildeburh could see that the items looked like roots and small dried fruits, but she couldn't identify them. As they added to the pot, the younger women sang:

> *Grant us warmth*
> *Grant us love*
> *Grant us you, Freyja,*
> *Mother goddess to all*
> *Wherever we are*
> *Grant us homes*

Bruna whispered, "Scylding maidens know they may have to marry and leave Hoc's hall to live with their new husbands. You, too, should be prepared for this, and we will teach you Freyja's worship so you may continue it wherever you may be."

She nodded solemnly, and as Hildeburh studied the lined and dark brown face, she realized that Bruna was the only old woman she knew who had never married. Bruna alone among the Scylding women was never referred to as a man's wife, mother, or daughter; she was simply Bruna. Bruna lived in her own burum, furthest from the main hall, and tended her own tiny garden in the back where she grew herbs but no food. She helped the women bringing babies into the world, tended the sick, and dressed the dying. The warriors called for her when their wounds were especially bad or when they needed dignity as they passed into the shadows.

Hildeburh had always vaguely expected that one day she would marry—but it never occurred to her that she might have to leave her home to do so, and she felt a wrench in her stomach like she was beginning to cry when she was distracted by the chant of the older women, grown stronger now, and she reminded herself that any marriage for her was well in the future and there were plenty of good young Scylding men who would be more than willing to marry the king's daughter. Hoc would not have to look away from home for a husband for her, she told herself.

The old women chanted more loudly, articulating the words that had been echoing in the background throughout the ceremony:

> *Take us*
> *We are yours*

> *In pain we know wisdom*
> *In wisdom we know joy*
> *We are yours*
> *Take us*

Hildeburh heard an odd sizzling noise as the contribution of the old women hit the boiling water in the kettle.

Then all the women relaxed. The formality dropped from their faces, and they laughed and chatted as they retrieved wooden cups from the large pockets Scylding women wore at their left sides. Hildeburh's pocket currently held her cup, tufts of carded wool, and a small hand spinner to make thread out of the wool, some dried meat left over from the winter stores, two shiny blue pebbles she had found in the harbor while waving goodbye to her father, and a small flat stone with magic runes and pictures carved on it to keep her safe from ailments and accidents.

The ceremony seemed to be over, and the older women motioned to the young girls to take their portions of the brew first. Most of the girls drank from their mothers' cups before they dipped their own, and as Hildeburh sipped from Freawaru's, she tasted a hot bitterness that changed oddly to a thick sweetness as the liquid ran down her throat. She felt warmth stretch into her chilled toes and fingers and her head lighten as she thought about the ceremony.

"Now I am really a woman, mama?" she asked.

Freawaru smiled at her. Hildeburh's mother was without question the most beautiful woman in Hoc's hall. Tall and blond, she braided her hair with golden cord to make it shine even more richly. She had a wide forehead and clear blue eyes. Best of all, in Hildeburh's eyes, was Freawaru's voice, which could be soft and gentle or commanding and stern. Even Hoc's warriors jumped when they heard the voice of their queen. Hildeburh, whose dark hair and brown skin came from her father, despaired of ever looking like her mother. "You are, sweetheart, and Bruna and I will teach you about Freyja and all her mysteries." The mention of Bruna reminded Hildeburh about her earlier musings.

"Did Bruna never marry because she is a priestess of Freyja?"

"Oh, yes. The priestesses of Freyja belong to the goddess alone and cannot share their lives with a husband or children. The men of our tribe think of her as a healer who has some connection to the gods, something like Caedmon's when he sings the songs of Odin and Tiuw. But Bruna watches over the growth of our tribe, our births and deaths. She is one of the most powerful to have dedicated her life to the goddess, as far as I know. She can bring the power of the goddess to the sick or the dying and to women bearing children. She knows the rhythms of the earth and can bless crops or take away a curse. She knows the old stories and the chants of the ceremonies and much else besides. Freyja has been kind to her."

"Will I have to get married and live far away from here?"

"You are full of questions this morning! I don't know about your marriage." Freawaru spoke the truth. She did not want her only daughter to pledge peace, the Scylding term for a marriage alliance that healed a breach between tribes. Hoc was a successful warrior, but successful warriors made enemies, and there were princes enough who would want to marry Hoc's daughter to keep him from raiding their lands. Freawaru had not discussed Hildeburh's marriage prospects with Hoc, preferring to think of her as a child. But Hildeburh was ten, she would be marriageable in two or three years, and now that she was a Freyja initiate she was definitely a woman, not a child. Freawaru reminded herself that she would have to survey the young Scylding men for a suitable husband for Hildeburh; if she didn't want Hildeburh to pledge peace, she would have to have a good candidate in mind when she broached the subject with Hoc. "Do you like Freyja's tea?"

"It tastes funny."

"The herbs of the goddess are a mystery to me. Bruna grows them in her garden behind her burum with her healing roots and plants. They do taste odd, but you will find in time that when the pain of childbirth begins to seem unbearable, Freyja's tea will show you love, not pain, and teach you that not only can you endure the pain but also learn from it and conquer it. We drink the tea on this spring morning, and Bruna makes more as the babies come through the summer."

"Did you drink it when you had me?"

"Yes. It made your birth wonderful. I was so scared at first; I didn't know what it would be like, and the tea showed me that the pain was nothing because you were coming."

Freawaru thought back to the late spring ten years ago when her water had broken in the back garden after days of mild but continuous clenching in her womb. The women had dropped their tools and helped her into her burum, which seemed empty in Hoc's absence. It was the largest of the outbuildings where the women and small children slept, with a great featherbed in one corner piled on top of fresh straw. Freawaru herself had plucked the geese and ducks for the bed she shared with the king. On the other wall was her loom, a great wooden frame with weights at the end of the warp threads and the woof threads bound onto shuttles, sorted by color and thickness to make patterns of both color and texture on hangings and royal robes. Freawaru's weaving-work decorated the walls, the rich hangings proclaiming that this was the residence of a queen, with gold threads and precious dye-colors in abundance. Hoc knew his lady's preference for rich fibers and always claimed them first from the plunder-pile, as was his right as king.

A large chest served as a table—it held winter blankets; other chests and trestles around the walls did double duty as benches when the queen had visitors, as she often did for weaving parties. Wedding and birthing dresses were made in the queen's burum; a generous queen, Freawaru would often contribute some of her fine stock to the communal effort. The women also met in the queen's burum to divide up the work of the season and to make decisions about planting the fields.

One woman had run to get Bruna; others had made her comfortable and helped her put on the birthing gown they had made so painstakingly together during the winter. The bodice was a loose wool with soft, treated deerskin on the inside so her swollen nipples would not be chafed. Freawaru herself had sewn the amethysts and garnets onto the shoulders where the seams met. Bruna had embroidered lucky symbols and runes onto the front, and every female over ten had put at least one stitch in the binding. The short skirt flared out to make walking easy; it tied onto itself at the back and onto the bodice at the top. When the time came, the women would untie the skirt from the bodice, spread the skirt on the floor, and Freawaru would squat above it. The women would hold her arms, Bruna would catch the baby and cut the cord, give the baby to Hild, and then wrap the bloody jelly of the afterbirth in the skirt to be buried in Bruna's garden. Freawaru remembered the mixture of pride and apprehension she had felt as they made the birthing dress, one in a series of dresses they made that winter for all the pregnant women. The bodices would be used again by the mother; for each baby, a new skirt was made.

The women opened the wooden shutters so the fresh sea air swirled in, taking away the sticky sweet smell of womb-water. When the pains started, they sang Freyja's songs to her, and then, when the pain became huge and terrifying and black and dizzying, Bruna gave her the tea, and Freawaru knew the peace in the very center of pain, knew the calm of a mother for the first time. Her baby was coming, and she knew somehow it was a girl, and Hoc would be disappointed, but she was happy, even joyous despite her pain, that it was a daughter and there was a link, a thread between them and Freyja would never separate them.

Hildeburh stood next to her mother, wanting to climb into her mother's lap like she had when she was a little girl. Freawaru's arm slipped around Hildeburh's shoulders and squeezed. "I just wish your grandmother could have been here for your first ceremony. She loved you so." Freawaru's mother, Hild, had been a happy woman. Her daughter had married her king, so there was never any question of losing her daughter to a peace alliance. Her burum was always full of children, Freawaru's friends and later

Hildeburh's, eating the honey cakes she stashed away for them, playing games she taught them with the round stones and the circles drawn in berry juice on the floor, and listening to her stories about Dagref, king before Hoc. Hild was short and plump; she grew flowers in her garden between the beans and tubers even though it meant extra work. Her daughter Freawaru looked nothing like her, looked like Hermod her father, and some Scyldings still wondered, quietly, what tall, stately, gorgeous Hermod had seen in dumpy little Hild, the flower-grower, who ended up marrying her daughter to the king.

Freawaru shook her head abruptly. The tea did it, she thought, makes the mind wander through the past, but usually only on good things, like a happy mother and a good birth labor. "We must go back soon," she said. "Eva and Jenga have had to watch all the young ones long enough."

The women heard the queen speaking and realized that authority was back in her hands. Bruna ruled the day no longer. They rose, getting ready to return to the hall and long houses in the lowland. Bruna gestured towards the girls. "You will sing with the maidens group next year and every year until you have a child. I will teach you your part this summer, but you must remember never to reveal it, even to any of the boys still too young to go to sea. Now let's return. Freyja knows we revere her, her earth, her sea, her power."

As they started down the hill on the rocky path, Hildeburh recalled what Bruna had said about the girls having to leave Scyldingland to live with foreign husbands. She shuddered and forced herself to think only about how she and Sunya could get Hnaef to give the care of the ponies to them.

Chapter Two

Hildeburh had been learning the minor healing rituals from Bruna for two years, in the late summer when she had just turned thirteen and the boats were sighted in the mouth of the harbor earlier in the season than expected. Sunya and Yrsa had watched the ponies on the hills and kept lookout for the men's return. An early return meant very good or very bad news—that Hoc's troop had so much plunder they didn't need to continue or that they were so badly injured and depleted they could not continue. Hoc had been known to send a small part of the fleet home in mid-August, loaded with booty, while the rest of the boats sailed westward for a final sally against the Picts or the Scots before returning to the Danish harbor. But Sunya reported ten of the twelve ships to the queen, and as the women abandoned their chores and rushed to the beach, each wondered whose ships had been lost, whose husbands and sons and pledged husbands-to-be were injured or killed, and who returned unharmed or with treasure.

Hildeburh carried the bags of bandages and the small chest of herbs and medicines for Bruna, whom she helped over the steep places on the path. She wished Bruna could walk faster. Hildeburh wanted to see her father and brother and also Hunlaf's son, Bjorn, with whom she had exchanged kisses by the well in the twilight before the men left. Hnaef, getting ready for his second viking journey, had said that Bjorn only liked her because she was the king's daughter.

But Hildeburh knew that was wrong. She and Bjorn liked the same things: racing the ponies over the hilltops, watching the great whales as they passed by the headlands on their mysterious autumn journeys, talking for hours about their ambitions for the future. He wanted to be a warrior-bard, like the Deor of old, and sing of his own and his king's great deeds. She wanted to learn to be a healer, ultimately finding just the right mixture of chants and herbs and magic so that winter babies wouldn't die and the wasting sickness couldn't kill. She still missed Anya. Hildeburh had begun helping Bruna the winter Anya died, and watching Anya slip away made her long to know the herbs and charms to stop such a loss. Oddly enough, she and Bjorn had become friends because of his sister's death, and she sometimes thought guiltily of their first kiss, only two days after Anya's burial. The following winter they had contrived to be together as much as they could.

"You want to make healing magic, and I want to make beautiful songs," he had breathed into her ear one cool day in early spring, and he had slid his hands under her loose smock and rubbed her breasts and gently bit the skin of her neck. "We are made for each other, Hildeburh, my princess," he had said, and she had felt that way too, enjoying the touch of his cool hands on her body.

Bjorn sang songs to her, Scylding songs of Caedmon's and foreign songs he had learned from the slaves; his songs told stories of gods and magic and giants and elves. When he sang of a beautiful princess, he always looked at her in such a way that she blushed and lowered her eyes, but he smiled at her, white teeth gleaming in his dark face, startlingly dark under his yellow-white hair. Bjorn's coloring marked him as chosen by the gods, Caedmon said, for those with white hair and dark skin lived lives of great glory or great tragedy.

Sometimes last winter, Hildeburh and Bjorn had huddled under a fur in a dark corner of the hall, listening to the bards, talking, his hands stroking her sides and her cheeks until both their bodies tingled and glowed and Freawaru would find them and sharply order them off to chores. Bjorn, at fourteen, was Caedmon's apprentice, but he still learned the skills all Danish men knew, in addition to harping and story-singing: repair of weapons, carving of drinking-horns, building and upkeep of the hall and the burum and the other outbuildings. Hildeburh was assigned but not yet formally apprenticed to Bruna, and she spent the winter checking on summer wounds slow to heal, helping women sick in the early stages of pregnancy, learning the healing chants and spells, and doing the general women's work of weaving, sewing, and spinning.

In the roaring, wet snows of the coastal Danish winters, the Scyldings did their work in the brief hours of semi-daylight, gathering in the dark of the mid-afternoon in the lighted hall for the only hot meal of the day, followed by songs and mead-drinking and socializing. This was the season of weddings, of weaving-parties and gossip. Men prepared their gear for the summer ahead; women wove and tended their children. Babies born the previous summer were starting to sit up and look around; other babies started growing in their mothers' wombs as the warriors spent long hours in their wives' burum and in the slave quarters. Danish winter was a time for haemod and stories and song and romance; Hildeburh and Bjorn, like many of the young people, had taken full advantage of it.

So as she stood on the beach, her first sight of Hoc standing in the prow of his dragon boat, Hnaef at his side, brought only momentary relief. Finally, she saw Bjorn, rowing on the starboard side of his father Hunlaf's ship with the walrus head carved at the front, and though his head was bandaged, he was obviously not badly hurt, or he wouldn't be rowing.

Hoc leapt from the bow into the shallows and helped drag the dragon boat onto the rocks. Then he lifted Hnaef from the foredeck and helped him through the swirling waters to Freawaru. Custom demanded a formal greeting from King to Queen as rule shifted from her to him. The Danes on the beach and in the neighboring boats listened.

"My Lady. It is with sorrow that I return early from our season's viking journeys, returning with injuries and losses rather than riches and victories. Two boats have been lost, those of valiant Herward and Bonstan and their crews, in a battle with Geats across the inner sea. The Geats took our companions' lives and much of our treasure; we escaped with almost nothing but what you see before you. The Scylding men will spend the winter healing and planning; next summer we will campaign against the Geats and recoup our losses."

"You are welcome with honor, my lord. Your people revere your courage in battle and give thanks that so many of our warriors have returned to fight for you again next summer," Freawaru answered formally.

This was the signal for the general chaos of landing to begin. Families were reunited, stories told, news exchanged in a raucous blur tinged with hysteria as the wounded finally could be treated. Hoc spoke quietly and urgently to Freawaru. "Hnaef saved my life—I'll tell you about it later—his right hand took a blow meant for my neck—look at it or get Bruna or something. I think it's bad."

Freawaru turned to Hildeburh. "Start tending your brother. I'll be there as soon as I can." As Hildeburh led Hnaef away by his unbandaged hand, Hoc folded Freawaru in his arms and she heard him say to her, "I can hardly believe we made it. I thought I would never see you again."

"Attend to your people, Hoc. We will talk later," Freawaru said, though she clutched his shoulders. It was always that way, that Hoc was king first and husband last, and Freawaru accepted that. The two of them separated, he to supervise the beaching of the boats, she to sort the wounded and what little spoils there were.

Hildeburh took Hnaef to the medical area that she and Bruna had set up in the cool shade of the sheer cliff rising up from the beach. His right hand looked like a club; Hoc had wrapped his undersmock around it and bound it with tar and twine. "It's been like this for four days, I think," he said thickly. "I can't really feel it any more."

Hildeburh looked over at Bruna. She was using her iron shears to cut the tunic off Wulfgar; it was stiff with dried blood, and parts of the cloth stuck in the wound as she removed it. Hengest, Wulfgar's son, and Hunlaf, Bjorn's father, held his shoulders and legs so that he wouldn't thrash from the pain, but Wulfgar was perfectly still, bearing the pain with honor.

As Bruna removed the last bit of cloth, the delicate scab came away as well, revealing a deep puncture wound the size of a child's hand. Hildeburh felt her stomach turn when a bluish cord, part of Wulfgar's intestine, slipped out of the hole in his side, spurting blood and foul-smelling fluid onto the stones. Hildeburh turned away. Bruna had no time to help her now.

She looked at the herbs in the chest and the piles of bandages Bruna had unpacked from the bags. "I will tend you myself," she said. "Bruna needs all her energy to save Wulfgar."

Hnaef did not answer. The high-spirited little brother who played with her and teased her was gone, replaced by this solemn young man, only a year younger than she. She felt his forehead. It was red, burning, hot, and dry. Hoc had packed the injured hand as best he knew—more than most warriors would get, for Hnaef was the king's son—yet Hnaef was burning with infection and fever. Standing on the foredeck for the entrance to the harbor had taken the last of his strength. Hildeburh was suddenly terrified. Her baby brother was probably going to die.

War wound infections were almost always incurable, Bruna had explained. When the wound had gone numb and smelled putrid and oozed green pus, she would drug her patient into near unconsciousness and cut off the limb with an old war-axe she kept for just this purpose. Then she cauterized the stump, using the flat side of an old sword heated in the fire. The oddness of these tools—the axe and the sword used to heal wounds caused by axe and sword—was not lost on Hildeburh. Bruna had said that the smell of pus and burning flesh and blood and vomit was terrible, but not as terrible as the pain of the man who had to lose an arm or a leg or a foot. Bruna told her that often the warrior begged her for a death-potion, wishing to go to Valhalla for Odin's feast rather than endure the horror of life as a half-man, a Dane who did not go on viking journeys.

But when the infection had spread, removing the wounded appendage did no good. When the patient's whole body was already stricken, there was nothing to do but wait and pray, administer the fever coolers, and then the tea of oblivion at the last. When Bruna showed Hildeburh the plant that helped the patient slide into sleep and then death, she had told her of Freyja's garden of death, of the visions of birth and flowering she had seen.

"Valhalla is a story told by men. They do not think of a place like Freyja's because they do not experience the gifts of birth. They think the world after this one is a big feast, like the ones we have in our own hall but much grander and more glorious. Death is not glorious, Hildeburh. It is ugly and putrid and painful. We try to make it easier, but death is hard. After death, our spirits can live in Freyja's garden, where there is no death, only constant birth and ripeness, the wheat grows continually, and the flowers bud and bloom with no winter interval. The leaves of oblivion take us there. If you decide to pledge yourself to the goddess, I will show you exactly how to use them. They are very, very powerful."

Hildeburh wasn't sure she wanted to pledge herself to the goddess; that would mean staying unmarried and childless for the rest of her life, and the things she and Bjorn did together in the fields and under the fur in the hall felt too good for her to decide that she could do without them. She was only thirteen and didn't have to decide until next year; fourteen was the usual age for pledging apprenticeship to a craft like metal-working, harping, or healing. Besides, she didn't want to give the leaves of oblivion to anybody, especially her own brother, and she shook herself as if to shake the thoughts of the leaves and of Bjorn from her mind. Then she went to work.

She laid her brother down on a long flat rock and gently placed his head on her folded cloak. "I'll be right back." She forced a smile. "Don't go anywhere." His only answer was a low moan.

She gestured to three of the slaves milling about on the beach. "Go up to the hall and get a strong, large fur," she ordered. "We will need it to carry your master's son to the hall." Then she sprinted to the herb chest and sprinkled a liberal amount of the strongest fever reducer in the bottom of her cup. As she poured boiling water over it, she sang,

> *Water take the fire away*
> *Hnaef and heat can't mix today*
> *Freyja, cool my brother*
> *Freyja, soothe my brother*
> *-earth, water, air-*
> *-earth, water, air-*
> *Freyja, take the burn away*
> *take the fire from there*

She climbed nimbly over the rocks back to Hnaef's makeshift bed. In the distance she could see Freawaru grimly setting the bones various warriors had broken, fixing the splints with bandages and tar. She obviously had no idea that Hnaef was near death, or she would be tending her son herself. Hoc didn't know either; both probably assumed it was serious but not fatal, that his young body would heal fast.

Hildeburh had come to the moment she had dreaded from the first minute she had seen the crude bandage on Hnaef's hand. Taking her knife from her pocket, she unsheathed it and started cutting carefully at the cloth crusted with blood and dirt and tar. When she had removed almost half of the cloth, the smell erupted from the wound and the bandage; her blood rushed to her head, and the cliffs wavered in front of her eyes as dizziness crashed over her. The odor of rank sickness and rotting flesh seemed to fill her whole body. She continued cutting, forcing the nausea and fear away, concentrating on the work of saving her brother.

The arm itself was swollen, the glands in the shoulder pulsing with the infection that streamed up the arm into Hnaef's trunk. It was streaked with deep red lines, and the flesh itself was a blazing pink, hot from fever and infection. The hand was barely recognizable as such, and Hildeburh turned it so that what had been the palm faced the sky and examined it. The sword cut must have split the hand right between the index and middle fingers, for all the fingers were intact, but the palm was sliced through all the way to the wrist. Hnaef's three outer fingers were grey and dead; half his palm was almost wholly severed from the other half still attached to his arm.

She took clean cloths, soaked them in boiling water, and waited briefly for them to cool. When she pressed the sides of the wound with the hot poultice, he moaned but did not wake, and this encouraged her. Perhaps he would not wake while she took half his hand off.

She went to the fire and moved the cauldron from the hottest point. As she held her knife so that the long part of the blade grew red and then white in the heat, she prayed silently to Freyja for guidance. Her words were not a formal chant but more of a hopeless pleading that echoed in her head. "Don't let him die, goddess, please, help me to heal him, goddess, please, guide my hand and my thoughts, goddess, please, don't let him die." When the length of the blade was white, she returned the cauldron to its place and hurried back to Hnaef.

Quickly, before she could let herself become squeamish, she trimmed the rotting flesh from his hand and the stink of the infected wound was joined by the smell of burning flesh. She cut away the three fingers and the sodden part of the palm, leaving the thumb and index finger intact. The heat of the blade formed a porous seal over the wound, and around it she packed another clean cloth, soaked in the boiling tea of berry roots to draw out the infection. She lifted his shoulders and poured small amounts of the fever tea, now cooled, into his mouth; she figured that if he swallowed half of it, that would be enough for the moment.

The slaves were finally returning, and when Hildeburh saw them she started loading her pocket with bandage cloths, berry root, and fever herbs. She held the bandage on the wounded hand as the slaves lifted Hnaef onto the fur and started up the path to the hall.

Later that autumn, when the danger was past and Hnaef was growing stronger, Bjorn wrote a song that he sang to her about a beautiful princess with magic hands who healed the prince, her brother, from a mortal blow he had taken, a blow meant for their father. Hildeburh heard in the song but remembered only dimly the long nights and days she had awakened in the hall next to her brother, who had burned with the fever of infection but finally sweated it out of his body. As she tended him, she had entered a trance-like state, something like the ones Bruna had told her about, and packed the root poultices onto his hand while singing in the language of the goddess. She remembered that she saw the garden, Hnaef riding a varicolored pony next to her through a forest lush with pines and flowers; she was floating on a balmy, fresh breeze that carried her through the woods next to her brother. Sun spangled through the tree branches, and the smell of the trees and the earth filled her very being until the force of the goddess pulsed through her hands into Hnaef's wound. Bjorn told her later she had chanted songs in a language none of the Danes had ever heard before, a language beautiful and rhythmic, and Hnaef's body had stopped jerking about in the involuntary spasms of fever, and had stilled and healed.

Shiny, hairless skin was growing over the place where Hildeburh had made the cut. Hnaef could not move his right index finger, but his thumb worked well enough, and he could press it against what was left of his palm to carry small objects. On Bruna's advice, Hoc had promised to let Hnaef begin sword work with his left hand after the midwinter feast; Hnaef had become again the energetic little brother Hildeburh remembered. Sometimes, in her sleep, she saw his face near death on the rocks of the beach, the sounds of moaning, wounded men and frantic women all around her, and she would thrash in her sleeping furs until Sunya and Yrsa woke her and she found herself in the girls' sleeping area in the dim firelight of the hall.

One night before the midwinter festival, a slave summoned her to Freawaru's burum. She reluctantly left the fireside, where she and Sunya had been making elaborate plans for their double wedding. While the girls were both too young to marry, the Danes were in the middle of wedding season, and three new burum had been erected in the frithstowe, the cleared area surrounding the hall. Sunya and Hildeburh had been designing complementary but not identical wedding dresses and contemplating strategy for convincing Freawaru to let them use her loom and some of her heavy gold thread. The identities of the grooms were of no little interest as well, and the girls had been giggling about Bjorn and the glamorously older Hengest when Hildeburh was summoned. She retrieved her cloak and made her grumbling way out of the hall and through the cold darkness to her mother's enclave.

She was surprised to see Bruna as well as Hoc and Freawaru there. "Is one of you sick?" she asked, before she even greeted them.

Hoc smiled at his only daughter. "Not to worry, Hildy. We are here to talk and rejoice, not to drink your magic potions. Come in, sit down."

Hildeburh crossed the room and sat cross-legged on one of the many chests that lined the walls. Still chilled from the brief walk outside, she kept her cloak snug about her.

"We are here to talk about you, Hildeburh," said Freawaru. "You are thirteen years old, on the cusp of adulthood. You are a king's daughter. And while the direction of your future will ultimately be chosen by Hoc your father, the three of us wanted to explain things to you and see what your feelings are."

Hildeburh nodded, staying silent, her heart thumping in her chest. *They know about me and Bjorn*, she thought. *They must be angry.*

"I had always assumed you would marry one of your father's thanes, Hildeburh, and raise your family here in Scyldingland, with the status of king's sister after Hoc has taken his final journey. But Bruna has spoken to us about the way you treated Hnaef's wound, Hildeburh, and she thinks that Freyja might have set another course for your life."

Bruna spoke from her place by the fire, where she was spinning undyed wool onto a hand spinner without looking at it, probably without even thinking about it. Hildeburh watched Bruna's hands as they moved unconsciously to mold the carded tufts into slender, strong strands ready to be woven. "What happened to Hnaef was most extraordinary, you know," she said mildly. "An infected war wound usually means death, and no one but you had any idea how serious it was. Not that anyone could have done more than what you did. Had I treated him, I would have done exactly the same. The main difference is that Hnaef would have died if I had treated him.

"The unusual part," and here Bruna put down her spinning and looked right at Hildeburh with her sharp, probing eyes, "is that you had no idea what you were doing. You performed surgical amputation, a procedure I had briefly described to you but you had never seen, and poulticed the wound with a unique combination of medicines that I have never used. In the four days that Hnaef hovered between life and death on the floor of the hall, we watched as you neither ate nor drank nor relieved yourself, did not speak except to chant in a language that we did not understand, and acknowledged nobody but your brother—not me, your mother, your father, your friends. It was, shall I say, very strange."

Hildeburh had known that something odd surrounded her healing of Hnaef, something that she didn't remember clearly. Bjorn sang of it, but only vaguely, and nobody talked of it, at least not to her, not even Sunya. Only Hnaef, who didn't remember much of it either, had treated her normally.

"What am I supposed to say?" asked Hildeburh. "I don't even remember most of that time, just feeling frantic that Hnaef was going to die. I can't explain what happened."

"But Bruna thinks she can," said Hoc, "and after this morning's hunt I am inclined to agree. I took the omens and prayed to Odin, as always. The indications were for a Northeast hunt, and we started on the trail of some elk. We came to a clearing, and I saw a white elk, a female, grazing the dead leaves of the white-barked trees, unaware of our presence. Then a male came as well, with shining antlers and a coat so dark it was almost black. I signaled that I wanted them both, because not only could we use the meat but I knew your mother would want those skins, with such unusual coloring. We fanned out, ready to close in for the double kill, when the male lunged toward the female elk to mount her. Ever seen an elk's penis, Hildy?" Hoc asked abruptly, changing his tone.

Hildeburh blushed and giggled. "They're long and skinny and pink. They look funny. I'd be embarrassed, if I were an elk."

Hoc's laughter filled the burum, and the others joined in. The elk's anatomy had evaporated the aura of seriousness and gloom, and Hoc proceeded with his tale in a gentler and more relaxed voice. "Well, he was embarrassed too, because before we could do anything, two gyrfalcons appeared from up in the hills. They swooped into the grove and started screeching at the male, who did look ridiculous. He bucked up onto his back legs, and his rod shrank back inside him, and the birds—I could see they were female—just drove him out. It was like they were protecting her.

"Once the male was gone, they started on us. We were down in the cover, behind snow banks, under bushes—they found us anyway. They stayed too close for arrows, too far for clubs, just dove and howled and screamed at us until the white female ran away and we were back on the cliff trail. Then they disappeared.

"We stopped at the rock altar on our return." Hoc was referring to the altar of Odin carved into the north cliffs by the sea, where sacrifices of goats and ponies and, sometimes, slaves were made to the All-Father to get good winds and success on viking voyages. Hoc often prayed there for guidance, as did many of the other men, especially Caedmon. It was generally understood that harpers had special contacts with the gods through their music; Hoc, as king, spoke for the Danes as he acted as high priest of Odin during the ceremonies of the midwinter solstice and the equinoxes. The men departed as soon after the spring equinox as possible, with its high tides and growing days, returning in time for the autumn ceremony. The midwinter rites were for the whole tribe; at the others, only the men were present. Hoc went to Odin's shrine whenever he needed supernatural advice. His father's bard, Cynewulf, had carved from the very cliffs the figure of

Odin hanging from the World Tree Yggdrasil, surrounded by the raven, the wolf, and the eagle, who attended him as he discovered the wisdoms of death and power and war. In a strange way, Hoc found comfort in that image of pain, as if Odin's knowledge could be shared with Hoc and make him a greater king, a more glorious warrior. Every spring, as he leaped into his dragon boat amidst the cheering of his people, Hrunting at his belt and his son and his thanes around him, Hoc knew that Odin favored him over other kings.

But his thoughts at the shrine that morning had not been of war. The white female elk was a sign of something at home, of women and haemod, and he had gone directly to Freawaru's burum upon his return from the unsuccessful hunt.

"Odin revealed to me only that this was a matter of women, not of war, and I came here to find Bruna and your mother earnestly discussing your future. So here we are. I shall speak last. Bruna?"

"Hildeburh, in less than a year you will have to make your decision about your service to the gods, most notably Freyja, wife of Odin All-Father," she inclined her head to Hoc, "and goddess of healing. That you will be a healer is not a question. You yourself have said that you wish to be a healer and learn Freyja's rites. But if you pledge yourself fully to the goddess—if you become her acolyte—you may not marry, you may not have children. You will live in my burum, learning her secrets, and take my place when I am gone.

"I say, Hildeburh, that I feel this should be your choice. The goddess spoke through you when you healed Hnaef from a wound that should have killed him. I believe that she has chosen you. She will make you a great healer, if you choose her service."

Hildeburh looked at Freawaru. The queen hesitated a moment before saying, "Hildeburh, I know only that whatever you choose, you will remain with me, my daughter, within easy distance of my burum so we can weave and sing and talk. If you do not marry, I will miss your children, and I will never be the one to wash my daughter's children fresh from the womb, to greet them into the world. But I will not miss that too badly. You will be here, and we can help Hnaef's wife raise their children, for there is no question that he will marry. I ask you only to remember, my daughter, that you have more than a year to decide. To pledge oneself to the gods is glorious but not a decision lightly made. Hoc?"

"Daughter, I feel much as your mother does. It has escaped none of us here—none of the Danes!—that you have formed a friendship with Bjorn, son of Hunlaf, apprentice to the bard. Bjorn is a good young man, son of a good thane. He will steer his father's ship with the walrus prow when Hunlaf starts to age. Bjorn would make a fine husband for my daughter. I would be happy to perform your marriage in two or three winters.

"But, I would also be willing to have a feast celebrating you as acolyte of Freyja, wife to Odin All-Father. You will not pledge peace and leave your people, for I do not need to move you about in a marriage alliance. My sword is enough, as the Geats shall see this coming summer season," he said grimly. "In a year, I will decide, but you must tell me what you desire. If I can, I will honor that desire and marry you to Bjorn or pledge you to Freyja."

As he finished speaking, Freawaru served her husband mead in a bronze goblet, and Hildeburh spoke for the first time. "I have a year?" she asked. All three of them nodded. "Well," she said, thinking of the double wedding she and Sunya had been planning, "I may be able to tell you before that year is out."

Chapter Three

"Trancing is the most difficult part of Freyja's mystery, child, just because it is so seductive. Often I feel I want to stay in Freyja's garden with its colors and scents, and not return to this world of blood and pain. And sometimes the goddess shows us horror too, makes us feel the wounds we tend and see the gore of battle where the wound was inflicted. You have already tranced, with the goddess' help, last summer when you healed Hnaef. But today I will show you the trance of boiling hands, which precedes every birth."

Hildeburh sat straight backed and alert on the floor of Bruna's burum. Early spring sunshine poured through the latticed shutters, and the fresh air was cool but welcome. Her legs were crossed, her bare feet happy to be free of the confines of winter boots. One long dark braid hung over her left shoulder, reaching almost to her belt. Because she didn't look like her mother, Hildeburh had always thought she was unattractive, but Bruna knew, watching her princess, that Hildeburh's beauty had a dark, wild edge to it that unnerved many men but drew others. Hildeburh's year of choice was almost over; in two months she would be fourteen and would have to decide whether to pledge herself to Freyja as acolyte or to marry Bjorn, son of Hunlaf.

"Pain and fire are very close, in the goddess' world. Women often describe the pain of birthing like a great flame devouring them from within. After the mother's womb water has broken, you go into the trance of boiling hands. You may not profane Freyja's sacred space of birth without this trance." Bruna looked sharply at Hildeburh. "If you do, the mother will probably, though not definitely, die in agony of fever and infection a few days after birth."

Hildeburh nodded but did not speak. Like the other women, she had seen Bruna perform the goddess's magic when she immersed her hands in the cauldron of boiling water. She licked her lips nervously.

"We will do it together, the first time. It is not hard. Come." They went out into the corner of Bruna's garden where she kept a fire going nearly all the time.

Unlike the other burum gardens, Bruna's grew no food. The women of the tribe sustained her with continuous gifts of produce and harvest; she feasted high in the hall with the whole tribe on winter days. As Hildeburh spent more time with Bruna, she gradually learned the uses of most of the plants and realized there was a system to the garden, so that plants that performed similar functions grew in the same areas.

They walked through the rows to the fire, over which Bruna had earlier hung a kettle of water. Little bubbles rose slowly from the bottom as they sat down facing each other next to the fire.

"Close your eyes," Bruna instructed. "Eventually you will be able to prepare yourself to trance almost instantly, but since this is your first planned trance, you will have to try, and it may take some time." Bruna thought back to the same lesson she had learned from her great-aunt Bryn, for whom she was named, priestess before her. Bruna's first trance had come with difficulty, some forty years before, and Bruna remembered her own fear and excitement that day.

"In a trance, you must open yourself to the goddess. You must allow her into your spirit, let her know that you desire to help this baby be born. Think first of life, and magic, and the gifts of the goddess. Think of the sweetness of her ripe grain, of the freshness of her clean water, the glimmering of the sun on her ocean, the perfume of her flowers. Taste the flower and the fruit, see the flower and the fruit, smell the flower and the fruit, open your soul to Freyja's power."

Bruna looked up. Hildeburh's eyes were already far away. *As I thought*, Bruna said to herself. *This one is a trancer*. Bryn had told her about trancers, priestesses who went easily into the world of the goddess, and could perform great magic because of it. I was right to press for Hildeburh to become my acolyte, she thought. She is a priestess born.

"I know you can hear me, Hildeburh, even in the world of Freyja's loveliness where you are now. I will do it with you this time, and then you will do it yourself. In the garden is a spring that flows from the very center of the earth, where the heat and pain are great as they are in any birth. Go over to that spring. Its waters are boiling hot, still steaming from the heat of the under earth tremors, but its hot water purifies those who love the goddess and her work—it does not hurt them. You are of the goddess. She does her work on earth through you. Put your hands in the hot spring, Hildeburh, to prepare yourself to do her service and bring new life into the world."

Bruna guided Hildeburh's hands into the water, being careful not to touch it herself. The steam alone reddened her hands, and small splashes made minute burns, deeper red spots, on her forearms. Hildeburh didn't flinch as her hands entered the boiling water. She swished them around three times; then Bruna helped her to remove them.

"Come back now, Hildeburh. Come back from Freyja's garden back to Bruna's."

Hildeburh shook herself and looked around, then down at her wet hands. "Did I do it? It worked?"

"Of course it worked. The goddess' magic always works, Hildeburh. It is only we who fail, when we do not prepare correctly or do not believe in her powers. There are other reasons for trancing, but this trance is the most common. You and I will enter the trance of boiling hands eleven times this summer, if you formally decide to become my apprentice. Now do it again, without my help."

Bruna watched Hildeburh's lips move. She mouthed, "Taste the flower and the fruit, see the flower and the fruit, smell the flower and the fruit," and as the breeze carried the tang of pine resin from the inland forest into Bruna's garden, the backs of Hildeburh's eyes dropped away. She sang, in a high, clear voice:

> *Ic this giedd wrece bi me ful geomorre*
> *minre sylfre sith. Forthon is min hyge geomor,*
> *tha ic me ful gemaecne bearn funde,*
> *heardaeligne, hygegeomorne,*
> *mod mithendne, morthor hycgendne.*

And then she plunged her hands into the boiling water.

Bruna just watched. The power was in this princess. Bruna had heard Bryn sing that song once, in the language she did not understand, but she knew it was the voice of a mother crying for her child, the voice of the goddess crying for the deaths of her children in the senseless wars that continued every summer. *Freyja does not care about treasure, about boar-head helmets and gift thrones and arm rings and swords with names*, Bruna mused to herself. She cries because her world, which should be full of grain and fish, new babies and beautiful weavings and baskets, was actually filled with warships and armor and ghastly wounds and painful deaths.

All women and children, Scyldings included, lived in fear of a summer invasion, foreign ships entering the Danish harbor when the men were away. They practiced, every year, dropping everything and running to the caves in the forest where extra supplies were stored. Destitution was preferable to capture and a lifetime of slavery. *Freyja's greatest mystery*, Bruna thought, *was why she allowed the killing and fear to continue. Perhaps to eliminate war, the goddess would have to eliminate men, she thought, and we need the men for haemod to make more babies.*

Hildeburh was coming out of her trance, her head jerking about as her eyes adjusted to the world around her and stopped focusing on Freyja's garden. "Now," Bruna instructed, "keep your hands pointed up, shake the water off them, and you are ready to check the readiness of the baby."

Hildeburh looked at Bruna. "How many babies have you brought into the world?" she asked.

"More than I can count," she answered with a laugh. "I have been birther for the Scyldings for over forty years. Some years we have only five or six babies. One year, the year Freawaru was born, there were twenty-two! That was early in my training, but I got a lot of practice that summer. One night there were three women in labor, and Bryn and I were alternating from one burum to the next, caring for each of the mothers. And in the midst of the chaos, Bryn looked at Eadgild, who was heavily pregnant with Hunlaf, Bjorn's father, and said, 'Don't you dare start until after these babies are born,' and Eadgild laughed so hard her water broke."

Hildeburh did not laugh, though Bruna did. "What did you do?" she asked.

"With four babies coming? I did my first delivery all by myself. And the grandmothers help a lot too. They may not know as much as we do about birthing, but they love their daughters more, and that alone gives them some of the goddess' power as they assist."

"Does each grandmother sing her own song to the baby?" Hildeburh found herself interested in all the details of the birth ceremony. She wanted to know what to expect, and didn't want to make any mistakes.

"The grandmother's song begins, 'Welcome to Freyja's earth, child of my daughter,' but after that she can add whatever she wants. Some women add nothing, some have made elaborate compositions that they practice before the birth. Caedmon's mother's mother, it is said, sang a song to him so beautiful he decided right then he had to become a bard."

"What did Hild sing to me?"

"Oh, I don't know, child. The birther never hears the grandmother's song; she is still working with the mother. We deliver the afterbirth, check for healing, pack on the snow, and make the tea to reduce swelling and pain. The grandmother takes care of the baby."

Hildeburh thought of the snowballs and ice chunks that she and Bruna had carefully stored in the coolest corner of the spring house just before the melt started. It had been a cold, damp, unpleasant job, but Bruna had told her that cold packs were absolutely necessary for the first day or more after a birth. They wrapped the ice in a pack for the birth area, and Bruna said that the cold stopped bleeding and reduced swelling.

"I miss Hild sometimes. I don't remember her very well anymore, just me and Sunya hearing her stories in the hall when we were little. I remember feeling cold and then being wrapped up in one of her furs and her holding me by the fire, but I don't remember what she looked like or anything."

"Well, Hild dreams with Freyja now. She is in the garden. I remember her joy at your birth and Hnaef's. She didn't put you down that whole first summer, except to let Freawaru feed you."

"She is in the garden?"

"Yes," Bruna said carefully.

"Could I trance to see her there?"

"I don't know. I cannot, though I know there are and have been priestesses who speak with the dead. If you pledge yourself to the goddess' service, I will teach you what I know about trances, but you will have to look for Hild on your own if you choose to try."

Later that day Hildeburh gathered shellfish on the south edge of the harbor. Sunya had wanted to come, but Hildeburh had put her off, wanting to be alone. Hoc and Freawaru watched her every move, waiting to see what she would choose. Bruna kept hinting at the tantalizing possibilities of magic and birthing. Bjorn was angry. It seemed like they never did anything fun together anymore.

Three days earlier they had ridden their favorite ponies far into the forest and stopped by a stream. While the ponies drank, Hildburh and Bjorn had lain on the grass on the bank. Two years ago they would have been looking for crayfish under stones and scaring fish with rocks. Now they just gazed into the sky and tried hard not to talk about what they both were thinking about. Hildeburh constantly felt a vague nausea, wanting to make Bjorn and Bruna and her parents happy, yet knowing that making herself happy was the most important thing. And she didn't know which she wanted more. She wanted it all. She wanted to be married to Bjorn and be a birther and healer. And she couldn't do both.

Hildeburh kicked gently at some shells fastened onto rocks at the waterline, then looked up the beach. The men were getting ready to leave. They had lined up the boats above the tide line and checked the repairs made last fall. They had chosen their ponies and corralled them near the harbor, leaving the others to roam the forested hills around the frithstowe. They had started packing the boats with hay and foodstuffs. Each warrior brought only one set of clothes and his weapons. Hoc's warband traveled with only the bare essentials.

Hoc had been hungering for spring, had been moody most of the winter as he brooded over the rout by the Geats, the injury to Hnaef, and the loss of last summer's plunder and supplies. Hildeburh knew the men would leave tomorrow or the day after at the latest. Hoc had a grudge to settle and treasure to reclaim. She had overheard him talking to Caedmon and Hunlaf about their strategy: they would sail straight for Geatland, ambushing the men as they left their harbor, and then waste their hall and their lands. They would take all their treasure and their women and children as slaves. Hoc could then stop at any number of major ports, Hedeby or Riga or Dublin, to sell the extra slaves before going on.

Hildeburh sat down on a large, flat rock. Her empty collecting basket was behind her, forgotten. She could see most of the harbor from her vantage point, and watch the waves lap in, darkening the sand and making the rocks shine. "Everybody wants me, and I don't know what I want," she said out loud to the sea. Nothing answered.

It was a day of magic, she knew, one of the two days a year when the day and the night were exactly the same length. Bruna had said it was auspicious to learn the trance on a magic day, and Hildeburh knew the men waited for good signs from Odin on this day before they left—otherwise Hoc would have had them off a week or more ago.

She was staring at an eddy in a tidepool as the incoming tide gathered strength and made ripples glitter in the wan sunshine. The shine dazzled Hildeburh, and before she was fully conscious of her desire to do so, the sounds of the world around her dimmed, the great cliffs and forests at the edges of her vision blurred, and she felt herself shrinking as she tranced into the tidepool, which had suddenly become an entrance to Freyja's garden.

"Adon, Adon," she heard female voices calling, and she turned to see a group of three girls, all naked, with their hair shining in Freyja's sun. Beyond them, a young man was lying in the shade on soft grass, and he watched them and smiled as they called to him and ran to join him. His bright white hair and dark skin reminded Hildeburh of Bjorn's, and just looking at his naked body made her feel like she wanted him to touch her the way Bjorn did; she wanted to join with him and feel his body in hers and on hers. She watched, yearning, as the girls reached him and lay beside him, each of them stroking the long flat muscles of his legs, his shoulders, his forearms. One ran her fingers through his shining hair as another kissed his lips and the third grasped his penis and stroked and then sucked it until it became huge and pointed up towards the treetops. Then she mounted him, straddled his hips with hers, and he smiled at the three girls and massaged their breasts as the third girl rocked above him, emitting cries of pleasure. At the climax, she called again, "Adon, Adon," before she slid off him to one side and lay on her back, breathing pleasure as she gazed into Freyja's sky.

On the Scylding beach, the seagulls soared on the sea air as Hildeburh moaned and twisted, now lying rather than sitting on the rock by the tidepool.

Hildeburh watched as the girls rose and formed a loose ring around Adon's body. His seed dripped down the leg of the one who had mounted him. They spun in their own small circles and sang,

> *Blithe gebaero ful oft wit beotedan*
> *thaet unc ne gedaelde nemne death ana*
> *owiht elles, eft blithe, blithe*

As they sang, the grass began to grow, shooting up its strands and embedding itself in Adon's body. Still with a dreamy smile, he lay watching the dance and the trees as the earth consumed him. It seemed to Hildeburh almost as if he grew into the earth, though she knew such a thing was impossible. As the grass grew over him, he sank into the soil, and when just a low mound in the shade marked his former presence, the three girls, still spinning, danced from Hildeburh's view into the forest beyond the garden.

"You have seen the death of Adon, Hildeburh, an interesting welcome to Freyja's garden for one so new to the craft." Hildeburh turned towards the voice and saw a short, plump woman sitting on a log. She knew immediately it was Hild.

"Grandmother!" she said. "You..."

"You were planning to trance and find me all day; you just didn't know it." Hild smiled, and Hildeburh realized she did remember what her grandmother looked like; how could she have thought she had forgotten?

"I look like you; I don't look like my father," was all she could say.

"Well, you were named for me, you know. But we haven't much time. Soon the men will be back at the beach to finish their packing, and I don't want them to find you trancing off into Freyja's garden."

"What should I choose, grandmother?"

"I chose Heremod, Hildy. Bryn thought I could have been a priestess, but I married your mother's father, and she trained Bruna instead. Haemod with the love of a man's body can be a wonderful thing, Hildeburh. Adon and his lovers showed you that. But the goddess wants you, Hildeburh, or you would not be here now in the spirit world so easily. She will show you the way; she will tell you your choice. But Hildy," and Hildeburh felt herself start to choke up as she heard that long-lost voice call her by her childhood name, "choose today. It must be today, not your birthday. I can hear them. Hoc and his men are coming to the beach. Goodbye, granddaughter. The goddess will keep you."

As the trance faded, Hildeburh heard Hild's voice:

> *Welcome to Freyja's earth, child of my daughter*
> *Trees sing your welcome*
> *Wild things sing your greeting*
> *May you be fresh as morning sea air*
> *New as meadow's bell flowers*
> *Constant as the sea*
> *Quick as a gull over a cliff*
> *Wise as a falcon in wind*
> *Deep as a mountain spring*

Daughter of my daughter
Welcome to Freyja's earth

With her birth song still ringing in her ears, Hildeburh turned blankly towards the sounds of the warriors making their way down the path from the frithstowe to the beach. Her head hurt, and there was a pleasant ache and stickiness in her loins from her sharing of the climax with Adon's lover.

Lying down in her undyed smock at the south edge of the harbor, Hildeburh was all but invisible to the men, who didn't see her. She half watched, half drowsed as they stowed their weapons at their places in each boat.

Scylding boats were light, fast, and masterfully organized. The captain of the boat steered from the back, where he could watch the actions of his men both in battle and on the sea. Hoc's dragon boat had a trap door storage area built beneath the rudder in which he stored the most precious parts of the plunder. Each of the ten warriors had his own bench, on which he slept, sat, and rowed; under the bench he stored his armor, his weapons, and his share of the plunder. In the center of the ship was the mast for the one large sail—Hoc's was striped with red and white—the iron plate on which a fire was built for cooking and for making fire spears soaked with tar, and the bay where the twelve ponies traveled in cramped discomfort. When he could, Hoc stopped the fleet to let the ponies graze and exercise; otherwise, they were taken from their pen only for charges up an enemy beach or forays into enemy territory for supplies or surprise inland attacks. Caedmon was Hoc's sailmaster as well as his bard, and he slept amidships next to the fire.

Hildeburh noticed Bjorn's white hair as he stocked his small section of Hunlaf's ship. Its walrus prow added bulk but made the boat an effective battering ram. Hunlaf's crew excelled at rowing, and when the wind was right they could get the walrus boat skimming over the waves so fast that it could smash the side of an enemy vessel and start it sinking.

She looked at Bjorn, whose quiet sullenness was evident to her even at this distance. He seemed angry, even vicious, as he stored his round shield, his leather corslet studded with iron, and his helmet. Bjorn was young, and no boar's head as yet adorned his helmet, though he hoped to have one as a gift from his father or his king before he turned twenty.

He wedged his plain but sturdy helmet under his bench—he rowed fourth on the left, a good place to learn the sailmaster's craft and watch his father at work, for Bjorn and Hunlaf both knew that Bjorn would captain the walrus boat one day. Then he rose and walked, with some others, to the north edge of the harbor, around the bend out of Hildeburh's sight.

All the men were making their way in that direction, towards the rock altar of Odin carved into the north cliffs.

Hildeburh saw baskets of fresh foodstuffs among the stores and realized that they were not leaving the next day; the men were leaving that night. The midday meal was over; Hildeburh had avoided the hall where Hoc had probably issued boarding orders. The men would sacrifice to Odin, and then the formal ceremony of leavetaking would happen as Hoc transferred his power on land to Freawaru.

Tomorrow would be the rites of initiation for the ten year old girls, then, Hildeburh thought, and the general sigh of relief that the hectic time of predeparture was over. Freawaru would call a weaving party in her burum, during which the responsibilities for the valley fields and the livestock would be assigned.

Hild had said Hildeburh had to make her choice today; somehow, those in the goddess' world had known before Hildeburh that the men would be departing. *It would be better*, she admitted to herself, *not to make him wait all summer to know my decision. He should sail knowing whether to expect a wedding in the autumn; then he'll have the summer to get over it if he won't.*

Would they marry in the fall? She thought about her trance, about the way her body had felt when she watched Adon and his lovers. The urgency of Bjorn's kisses had grown over the winter, and she knew he wanted to be in her bed as much as she wanted him there. She thought of having her own burum, maybe next to Sunya's, who was already pledged to Hengest for next fall, and raising her children next to her friend, close to her mother. She imagined making a featherbed for herself and Bjorn, weaving them blankets, kissing and licking his body all through the long winter together.

I could still help Bruna, she thought. *I could be a minor healer, not a priestess, kind of how Freawaru is, and still marry.*

No more trancing, however. Healers who were not priestesses of Freyja set bones and tended wounds, mixed some herb teas and treated aches in the joints and stomach disorders. They didn't perform surgery, and they did not deliver babies. *But I can live with that*, thought Hildeburh. *I'll have my own babies instead of helping along someone else's.*

Hildeburh sat up and took a deep breath. The beach was empty, the last warrior having gone around the bend of the cliff a few minutes before. *I guess I've decided*, she said to herself. *Just like Hild. Sex and babies over trances and magic. Hoc and Freawaru will be pleased.*

She felt a rush of pleasure as she thought of Bjorn's face. His white teeth would gleam in his dark face when she told him his princess would be waiting for him on his return from the viking summer.

She stood up, picked up her empty basket, and started back towards the path. Halfway there, she decided to go directly to the top of the beach and wait for Bjorn there; he would come by the boats from the ceremony for Odin. She was heading towards the northern ridge when the wind brought an odd howling sound to her ears.

It wasn't wolves, whose howls she knew. It was the sound of a chant to Odin, and it made her skin crawl. The women and children always stayed in the frithstowe during the men's rituals; in almost fourteen years, Hildeburh had never been close enough even to hear what they did in their ceremonies. Women are not welcome at the mysteries of Odin, Caedmon always told the children, because battle and knowledge are men's things, and Odin All-Father is god of both. He had always accompanied this explanation with a baleful glare that forbade any questioning, especially from young girls like Sunya and Hildeburh, who had enough of their own knowledge to know that their mothers knew many, many things.

Hildeburh started as a high-pitched wail joined the howling. She couldn't place the sound at first, but then realized it was the wordless cry of a woman. It made the hair on her arms stand up, and her throat thickened with revulsion as she heard, for the first time, the sound of terror.

Later, she would think to herself that Freyja must have possessed her, for Hildeburh went towards the sound, disobeying her father, tribal custom, and the All-Father himself as she went to spy on the spring ceremony to Odin, burning with a sickened desire to know what they did to a woman to make her cry like that in the mysteries.

She carefully climbed up the northern hill of the harbor, looking for a place where she could see over the ridge to the north cliffs without the men detecting her. She settled behind a scrub pine next to a large boulder; she could see through the tree's branches, but the shadow of the rock darkened her hiding place and screened her from the group of men.

Below, she could see the top of the figure of Odin carved from the rock. On the ground before the sculpture was a large stone slab, brown-grey, flat and rectangular. Caedmon stood between the cliff wall and the slab; he wore a cloak of elk skin that Hildeburh had never seen before. Mystical runes and drawings were dyed onto the back of the cloak, and Hildeburh recognized, even from a distance, the figure of Odin hanging from Yggdrasil and some of the runes of power.

Hoc stood at the foot of the slab, naked but for his iron circlet. His chest and back had been painted, probably by Caedmon, with many of the same runes and magic circles. The rest of the Scylding men, in their usual smocks and breeches, formed a half circle around the altar, the king, and bard.

The wailing stopped. Hildeburh had avoided looking at the altar, purposely looking around it, but as the sound trailed off and stopped altogether, she forced herself to look at the woman. She was one of the slaves taken in raids against the Eirans two summers previous, and her tangled red hair formed a crown around her head as she lay on the altar. Like Hoc, she was naked.

The slave had worked in the hall kitchens, and spoke a language markedly different from the Scyldings'. It was hard to get her to do anything; she refused to learn the language of her masters and seemed to have a stubborn streak. But Hildeburh felt nothing but pity and horror for her now.

Caedmon must have drugged her, for her breath came fast and shallow while her open, unseeing eyes stared towards the grey sky. Her shrieking had stopped as the drug took effect. She made no resistance as Caedmon took her wrists and bound them above her head.

The howling began again, setting Hildeburh's teeth on edge. The men flung their heads back and howled to the sky, for Odin was a sky-god, and they sang to him in the language of the wolf, the beast of battle and blood. Underneath the howls, Hildeburh heard Caedmon chanting as he picked up a large clay jar that had stood next to the cliff. He walked around the circle, pouring a dark liquid into the mouths of the howling warriors. By the time he got to the end of the line, the first man was jumping up and down, howling louder than the rest. The others followed as the drug and the magic took hold, until each man seemed about to explode with energy, rocking, bouncing, and howling.

Hildeburh watched Bjorn, and hardly noticed when Caedmon poured some of the liquid onto her father's penis and then into his mouth. Bjorn's eyes were wide with the fervor of the moment; he raised his arms above his head and thrust his hips back and forth as he howled his frustration to his god. His white hair shone in the dull light of the afternoon, and Hildeburh thought he looked like a god himself.

A movement on the altar distracted her from Bjorn. Hoc had pulled the slavegirl roughly towards him on the stone, and red streaks marked where her back bled as he moved her. She lay inert as he pushed her thighs apart. His engorged penis was black with the dye of the magic that Caedmon had poured upon it, and as Hoc slammed himself into the girl, her blood and the black dye mixed in a gruesome swath on her white skin. He threw back his head and howled to Odin, calling down spirits of evil upon the Geats and all who dared oppose him, willing his warriors to follow him in all his greatness as they gloried together in their worship of Odin.

Hildeburh watched as each of the warriors took his turn with the slavegirl, who remained unseeing throughout the ritual. They tore off their clothes as they howled and stamped, and Caedmon kept crying, "Berserker!" in a deep voice as the men pounded a rhythm on the earth that kept time for the warrior pumping on top of the slave.

When Bjorn's turn came, Hildeburh turned away and vomited.

The chant changed, and she turned back, determined to see it through. *If I've already broken the law*, she thought grimly, *I might as well see it all and know what they do.* The men were still naked, their flaccid penises coated with blood and seed, their own and others'. They squatted among the rocks around the altar, the chant quieter and somehow more menacing than the howling. As Hildeburh listened, she realized they were repeating one word, *sweorcan*, drawing it out and layering its syllables upon one other so that the holy word for darkening and angering took on an ominous and vengeful tone.

Caedmon, naked under his elk cloak, approached the altar. He raised his face to the sky and sang:

> *Sky-Father Odin, Glory is Yours*
> *The wolf fights for you*
> *The raven gathers for you*
> *The eagle counsels you*

Sky-Father Odin
Take this woman
Take this goddess
Take this softness and weakness and spite
Make us warriors
Make us sailors
Make us berserkers,
Hard and strong and dark as night.

The men started howling again, softly at first and then louder. When the howling drowned out his song, Caedmon drew a knife from underneath the elk cloak and slit the woman's throat. He plunged his hands into her neck, filled them with the woman's blood, smeared the blood on his face and on his robe. He moved through the men, cuffing each warrior across the forehead with his bloody hands. As he was anointed with the blood of the sacrifice, the warrior ran to the sea. Hildeburh began to creep backwards slowly when all the men, her father and the bard included, were in the water, purifying themselves for the summer ahead.

Shaking, she made her way across the headland, cutting back to the frithstowe without going near the path. *I have to avoid them all*, she thought, *and they'll be in the hall or in the kitchens*. She slipped through the back north gate and climbed over Bruna's fence into her garden. Silence enveloped her. She lay down among the lavender and wished she were dead.

She must have fallen asleep, because Sunya was shaking her. "Hildeburh, where have you been? I looked on the beach and everywhere for you. Come on, it's departure day. They'll be leaving soon." Sunya's urgency faded away when Hildeburh sat up. "What's wrong with you? Are you sick? I'll get Bruna."

"No, Sunya, don't. Help me. I'll be alright." Hildeburh leaned over and retched, yellowish bile coming from her empty stomach. "Let's go."

Sunya helped her to stand, and they set off at a half-run for the beach. They hurried along the side of the hall to the main gate and the path, catching up with the last of the Scyldings making their way to the beach for the ceremony of departure.

Hoc was still checking the fleet, looking resplendent in his short fighting tunic and swordbelt. There was no trace of Odin's mysteries about him; he looked just as he always did this day, and Hildeburh started to wonder if she had dreamed him thrusting himself into that servant girl and reveling in her blood afterward.

She slid through the crowd of women and children and made her way to the walrus boat. Bjorn did not see her; he was bent over his bench, checking his sword blade. She touched him lightly on the shoulder. "Bjorn," she said gently and happily.

He turned toward her, and she recoiled as if she had been struck when she saw the echo of a smear of blood on his forehead that the sea had not washed completely away. In that instant, her mind changed irrevocably, and she knew she could never marry anyone, could never love and kiss and delight in a man who could participate in Odin's mysteries.

"Bjorn Hunlafing, today Bruna has tutored me in the mysteries of Freyja. I have entered into a trance and seen the world of the spirits and the goddess. Much as I have loved you, I found today that the goddess calls me and I must not refuse. I wished you to know this now. I am sorry, Bjorn," she said as formally as she could.

Hunlaf was behind his son and had heard all that she said. He had nursed hopes of his son marrying the king's daughter, and he cursed under his breath. Even he, however, was surprised at the venom of Bjorn's answer.

"May your goddess curse you, Hildeburh," he whispered spitefully. "You belong with me, not with her. You know that. So go and hide with your potions and spells. I'll find someone else."

Hildeburh leaned forward so that only he could hear her. "Bjorn," she said softly, "there's still blood on your forehead." Then she walked away, up the path to the frithstowe, not caring who saw that she flouted the ceremony where Hoc handed Freawaru his sword and charged her with the keeping of his hall and his lands and the Scylding women and children until he returned. She wanted nothing to do with warriors. She had made her choice.

Chapter Four

Hildeburh stood in the doorframe of Hoc's hall. The enormous deer antlers, as wide as she was tall, hung over the doorway, proclaiming to all the hunting prowess of the hall's owner.

In the twilight of early autumn the Scyldings had lighted their hall with torches. Hildeburh could see the entire length of the hall to the other end where her father's imposing gift-throne stood. It had been carved for Scyld out of the rock of the sea cliffs, and its runes and figures told stories of kingly greatness, fighting skill, and open-handed generosity. Hanging behind the throne was one of Freawaru's weavings, showing Hoc in his dragon boat, surrounded by sea creatures and swirling waves. In the borders of the hanging the Scylding women had stitched separate scenes of the king's life: giving treasure, building the hall, naming his children, capturing slaves, accepting tribute. When Hoc died the weaving would be burned with his body in the dragon boat at the entrance to the harbor.

The Scylding warriors and women sat on the benches that lined the hall, all dressed in their finery. The women wore their best dresses with jeweled shoulder clasps and precious necklaces. All the warriors wore at least three golden arm-rings above the elbow, testimony both to their bravery in battle and to Hoc's generosity. Fine swords hung at jeweled belts; sturdy helmets decorated with the figures of boars perched on the benches next to the warriors. The men's tunics were dyed blue and deep red, each slit up both sides to reveal the breech wrappings beneath. Some men and a few women wore torques, ceremonial collars of iron or even silver that were a mark of the king's highest favor.

Hildeburh couldn't focus on the people lining the hall. "Freyja. For strength," she whispered to herself and mouthed the words of a song to the goddess, willing herself to look into the torch-lit hall.

Hoc and Freawaru emerged from behind the magnificent weaving, resplendent in their finery. Hoc wore his golden circlet studded with onyx and amethyst over his grey hair. An embroidered deer skin patch covered and decorated the place where his left eye had been. His beard partially hid his gold torque. Freawaru had just finished weaving his blood-red tunic, which was cinched about his warrior's waist with a leather belt, studded with quartz. His great sword, Hrunting, hung in its ceremonial scabbard, leather worked with gold cord.

Sunya put her hand on Hildeburh's elbow. "Pay attention," she hissed. Hildeburh started as if Sunya had somehow woken her up. She felt almost as if this marriage wouldn't happen if she didn't pay attention to it.

And she hadn't. All through the summer she had worked in Bruna's garden, learning more deeply the secrets of the herbs, chants, and stories, continuing her training as Freyja's priestess. The other women had made the dress which she now wore, made from the softest lambswool and dyed with the rare yellows and pinks of the spring shellfish in the bay. Over the summer, Freawaru's bruises and broken ribs had healed from the beating Hoc had given her, and the wedding plans had gone forward.

As Caedmon began a song telling the story of the Princess Hildeburh's wedding, Hildeburh remembered the previous spring, before the men had left, when a boat from Frisia with an eagle's head for a prow had been sighted in the harbor. The Frisian envoys had disembarked and lain their war gear in gleaming rows along the rocky beach and then stepped back to show their peaceful intentions. Their leader, Handschue, had asked for an audience with Hoc. The Frisians had been escorted to the hall with all correctness, and at some point during the course of the banquet that followed, Handschue had given Hildeburh the amber and gold necklace she was now wearing as a gift from Finn, his prince. Handschue and Hoc had agreed that Hildeburh would pledge peace between their tribes by marrying Finn.

Hildeburh had been stunned. Not, as Caedmon's song stated, by the overwhelming beauty and grandeur of the betrothal gift, but by her father's willingness to pledge an acolyte of Freyja in marriage.

Since that spring morning when Hildeburh had first participated in the annual welcoming of the goddess, her proper place as Bruna's assistant had become more and more evident to her people. Even the Scylding men, who thought of Freyja only as Odin's wife, noted that Hildeburh's hands were gentle and sure when the men needed their wounds tended. In the three summers since she had seen Odin's rites, Hildeburh had assisted Bruna continuously. Two summers before, Bruna had begun to let her attend many of the uncomplicated births, and Bruna had slept soundly in her burum as Hildeburh woke all night with the laborer and her chosen companions, brewed the tea, and tended the mother after the birth. When the tiny infant came on time, head first, the priestess' job was easy; Freyja and the mother did the work.

Bruna had allowed Hildeburh to assist at the more difficult births, the ones where the baby was upside down and wanted to come feet first, the ones where the mother's womb was weak and the baby was dying from an overlong pregnancy, and the ones where the baby wished to birth too soon. Bruna made special teas to start or still the contractions; one horrible night last winter in a spasm of blood and fever Yrsa had given birth to an exquisitely tiny and deformed little creature that looked like a fish. Though Bruna had explained later that the baby had simply not had enough time to grow in its mother's body, Hildeburh had been horrified, sure that Yrsa had had haemod with a god of the sea.

In the autumn when Hildeburh was fourteen, Hoc had agreed that she could live with Bruna and take over the healer's duties as she aged. As a healer, Hildeburh would remain unmarried among the Scyldings for her whole life, living with honor as a priestess of birth and healing. Hidleburh had seen the sorrow and bitterness in Bjorn's eyes at the banquet that autumn that celebrated her as Freyja's acolyte, but her own happiness eclipsed his distress. She knew by then that she was born, like Bruna, to the mysteries of birth and blood and healing.

Caedmon sang of the battle, her sixteenth summer, between the Scyldings and the Frisians when Hoc lost his eye but won the day, returning to his harbor with all but one of his boats. Among the plunder was the necklace Freawaru wore, a fine gold mesh braided with gems and exquisite corals. Folcwalda's people had been scattered. Since this was a feast of allies, Caedmon sang too of Frisian bravery, the sinking of the Scylding ship, the glory of the deaths of those who had fallen in the service of Folcwalda their king. The marriage of the Frisian prince and Scylding princess would bind these two brave and glorious peoples, Caedmon sang, and as he launched into verses celebrating Hildeburh's beauty, the company gathered in the hall turned to look at her, standing in the doorway awaiting the first part of her marriage to Finn as a pledge of peace.

She was beautiful, in her wedding dress, her skin still brown and her dark hair still streaked red gold from the summer sun. Earlier in the afternoon, Freawaru, silent and smoldering, had braided it in her burum, wound pink and yellow cord and long stemmed flowers into it. The queen did not like this marriage; all the Scyldings knew it. After Hoc had beaten her into acceptance last spring, he had taken to sleeping in the hall with the warriors rather than in the queen's burum. Hildeburh still felt nauseous when she thought about it, the argument that everyone heard. She had been sitting by the well with Sunya and Hnaef and Hengest and some others when the queen's voice had carried through the evening air and said to Hoc what everyone was thinking.

"You cannot marry her off! She is pledged to the goddess. If we take her from Freyja, the babies will not come, the crops will not grow, the Scylding line will wither and die like wheat in a drought. You cannot do this."

Hoc's voice rumbled and carried deeply through the shadows. "Don't you tell me, woman, what I can and cannot do. They have made a good offer for her, and the marriage saves me from fighting them again this summer. Do you hear me? They half-blinded me, and I don't care what Caedmon sings, we almost died. All of us. If Bjorn hadn't downed Folcwalda's horse, we all would be in Odin's shadows now. They are our match. We can't beat them again, and they might not be able to beat us, and we would all die trying. This marriage is the only way to avoid a summer of death. If we avoided Frisia, they would come looking for us. I know Folcwalda; he won't let a loss lie, not without honor—like the body of a princess to seal a peace bargain. Now don't bring it up again, I warn you. My mind is made up. Bruna can get another of the girls to help her. It was my mistake to let her be an acolyte when I might need her later to pledge peace." He spoke with kingly finality in the voice of a man who is used to being obeyed.

"The goddess will curse us." All the listeners by the well had jumped to hear Freawaru's voice again. Even Hildeburh had assumed that the discussion was over, that Hoc had explained himself—something he rarely did—and the decision was made. "The kingdoms and fighting of men are not her concern. You kill each other while she brings life. She will not let a killer like you take her priestess. And I cannot bear that you would take my only daughter from me."

Then Hildeburh and her friends had fled as Hoc's roar of rage had filled the sultry evening air. Hildeburh and Sunya ran up the path to the pony shed away from Freawaru's screams and the sound of her body crashing into the walls of her burum as Hoc struck her again and again. It must have been many times because later that night in the hall when Hoc had abruptly told her to go to her mother, Hildeburh had seen her mother's face a bloody mass of bruises and lacerations from her own teeth; most of her ribs were broken as well. She had helped her mother with compresses and bandages, wrapped her chest gently in the finest, lightest cloth she could find, and ordered her to lie still. She could not protest the next morning when Hoc insisted on having the tribe witness Freawaru's agreement to the betrothal and her promise that Hildeburh would be ready for marriage in the fall, after the men returned but before the sea locked the harbor in with ice. Many of the Scyldings had lowered their eyes when their queen tottered to the circle before the hall on the arm of her daughter, her face unrecognizable. Freawaru had tried to hold her head up and speak clearly.

"I swear to you, my King, before my people, that my daughter Hildeburh will be ready for marriage upon your autumn return. Any distress I have felt about this matter has been stilled. Your wishes will be obeyed in your absence." Without waiting for any response, Freawaru had turned away from the gathering and her husband and returned to her burum. She did not emerge until after the men were gone. Hildeburh had taken Hoc's sword and handed it back to him at the departure, accepting responsibility for the tribe and lands that summer. With no Frisians to worry about, Hoc had pointed his ships towards the land of the Saxons. He had heard that the Saxons made wonderful swords and mailcoats but were not skilled in using them.

Sunya nudged Hildeburh forward. Caedmon was singing the entrance of the bride.

She walked down the center of the hall towards her parents, Hoc seated rigid-backed on his rock throne, Freawaru beside him holding an enormous golden cup. Caedmon's voice stopped, but his harp did not, and the airy sound of the strings gave her something to focus on as she made her way by the silent Scyldings and the group of Frisians who had come as witnesses to this part of the marriage. She and Finn were to be married twice, before her gods at her home as well as before his in Friesland.

She had met Finn, of course. Shortly after the Scylding men returned from the viking summer with loads of Saxon plunder and slaves, three eagle-prowed ships had sailed into the harbor, bearing the groom and his wedding party and gifts for the bride and her family. Sunya had come to get her from Bruna's garden, and thus she had met her future husband, who had asked to see her immediately, with dirt under her nails, wearing only an undyed work smock. Finn was short and broad though not at all fat; his bulk gave him an aura of incredible physical strength. He wore a circlet of flashing silver on his forehead; in their simplicity, his black tunic and leather belt proclaimed him to be a businesslike warrior prince. She had liked his plain but honest face well enough, but had not been especially attracted to him. If he had not been there to marry her, she would have welcomed him with honor due from a king's daughter to another king's son and then ceased to think about him.

Finn had spent most of the intervening days with Hoc, hunting the inland forests and riding the Scylding ponies. Part of Hildeburh's dowry was to be a stallion and three mares, the choice to be agreed upon by all. In the afternoons, while the hunted beasts were prepared and cooked for that night's feast, Finn and his Frisians had joined Hnaef and the other young Scylding men to go to the slave quarters for haemod with the women there. Hildeburh sensed the distaste of many of the Scyldings—while lying with the slaves was the right of any man of the tribe or its guests, Finn seemed to have no idea it would be more appropriate, somehow more seemly and kingly, to spend that time with Hildeburh.

The slaves gossiped, too, in their odd slave language of foreign tongues mixed with the language of the Scyldings. Hildeburh looked at the man now standing next to her father, watching her approach, and knew what she had to expect during her first haemod later that night. A workmanlike performance with a long groan at the end, then he rolls over and goes to sleep, even in the daytime—that was the smirking story the Jutish slave told to Hildeburh and her friends.

Finn wore finery as well, having exchanged his utilitarian belt and scabbard for more elaborate, tooled versions. He wore a gold circlet much like Hoc's except it was studded with gems Hildeburh didn't know. They were small, round, and gleaming lustrous white. When Hildeburh stood directly in front of the gift-throne, Caedmon's harp strings stilled, and Sunya stepped back and melted into the crowd of Scyldings. She had escorted her friend on her wedding walk, as Hildeburh had done for her three autumns before when she had married Hengest.

"Hildeburh." Hoc's deep voice rolled and echoed through the massive wooden hall. Torchlight gleamed on his raiment so that Hildeburh found it hard to look directly at him. He had taken her from her goddess; he had beaten the mother she adored; and yet she still loved him. She remembered him teaching her to ride the ponies, to hold onto their thick manes and use the muscles in her legs to steer wherever she wished to go. She remembered the way he had always spoken to her like an adult, even when she was a tiny child, and how he taught her and Hnaef to dig for clams on the beach back when his hair was black as hers. In the winters he had told her stories in Freawaru's burum, and before she left to sleep with the other girls, he would tickle her with his beard, and in the mornings when she came back, he let her play in the furs of that wonderful featherbed while Freawaru brought him warm mead or tea.

"I speak now not only as the father who cares for you and as the king who commands you but also as the priest of Odin that I am by right of kingship. When I lost my eye, I found much of the wisdom of Odin in the blackness. Like Odin, I am blind in one eye; his priest sees into the power and workings of the All-Father. He is the god of all; he controls death and battle. I pray to him that one day I might sit as a thane at his feast in Valhalla to be served by Valkyries and rewarded for my time here on earth, serving him.

"I lost my eye to a Frisian, but I see now the loss was well worth it. For now we have a wedding feast rather than a raging battle; we have an exchange of gifts rather than a taking of plunder. Odin is content. His battle lust rages no more between Scyldings and Frisians.

"And so, as priest of the All-Father, as King of the Scyldings, and as father of the bride, I proclaim the marriage of my daughter to Finn, prince of the Frisians. To Finn I give her, untouched by any man, with three mares and a stallion, with her loom, and with three dowry chests full of cloth. She pledges peace between our peoples, who will fight no more but instead feast and rejoice in our good fortunes." Hoc took Hildeburh's hand and led her to Finn. He placed her hand in the Frisian's, which felt much the same as her father's: large, calloused, warm. Her own thin fingers were icy cold but clammy with a nervous sweat. Their first touch, she thought.

Hildeburh looked at her mother, who through the song and Hildeburh's entrance and Hoc's speech had stood still, looking like a sculpture of one of the Valkyries herself. Her stately stillness lent an aura of elegance to the proceedings, but her sorrowful eyes were not those of the usual bride-mother's. Freawaru was thinking of her own sorrow, to be a mother with a daughter far away, to be queen of a people cursed by the goddess for the theft of her acolyte. She thought of her daughter's probable misery, away from her home and all her people, in the arms and the control of a husband who lay with slave girls even on his wedding day. And finally Freawaru was sad remembering her own wedding day, a day of tribal happiness as the beautiful daughter of the young king's thane pledged marriage to the king. Hild had stood and smiled with pride as Hermod had put Freawaru's hand in Hoc's, and Hoc was dashing with the dark good looks of his youth, a contrast with Freawaru's bright beauty. No happiness like that awaited Hildeburh, Freawaru was sure.

The month since the men had been home had not been easy. Since she was no longer bleeding regularly, Freawaru had the right to deny Hoc her bed, but she missed the companionship they had built together in her burum, speaking about the children, the tribe, the organization of

their people, their lands, their animals, their boats. Hoc
was a fighter, not a manager, and Freawaru's suggestions
from those discussions often echoed in the king's orders
to his people. While the men were away, the queen ruled;
since they had been back, she had done little but weave
in her burum, pondering her own and her daughter's
sorrows, wishing a freak storm would sink the Frisian
party before it arrived for what she was sure would be a
disastrous wedding and marriage.

Finn's voice, higher and clearer than Hoc's, accepted
Hildeburh. "Hoc, son of Dagref, king of the Scyldings,
and priest of Odin All-Father whom we call Woden, I
gladly take your daughter back to Friesland as my wife and
later as my queen. Our marriage makes peace between our
noble peoples. I leave for you, my bride's father, the coral
necklace on your queen's neck and these." Finn proferred
a small bag, smaller than his fist, fastened with a polished
metal clasp. Muttering in the hall was silenced by a glance
from Hoc, but the veins in his neck bulged, and everyone
knew that Finn had just insulted his new father-in-law.
The necklace Freawaru wore had been taken as rightful
plunder during the battle the season before. It was no gift.
Finn had no right to pretend it was part of the marriage
settlement. Courtesy dictated he not even notice it.

Hoc seemed to have decided not to notice the insult. He
opened the pouch and poured the contents into his hand.
His huge palm filled with the same stones that adorned

Finn's circlet; in addition to the gleaming white stones, there were pink, blue, and even green tones in some of the unknown gems.

"These are pearls, and they grow in the shellfish that live in the bay of Frisia. Our young girls harvest them in late summer; only one in twenty contains a pearl, and all pearls belong to the king. My father Folcwalda sends these to you.

"In Frisia, the old women tell a story of a beautiful necklace worn by Neursa, a sea goddess. One day Woden came upon her in our harbor, wearing the necklace as she sunned her gleaming body. When she refused his advances, he took her by force, and the necklace burst, and she hid its pearls by magic in the shells of the oysters."

"They are precious and beautiful, worthy to adorn a goddess. Thank you, husband of my daughter," said Hoc formally. "The riches of Hildeburh's marriage will be shared among the tribe, just as the peace she pledges is." Hoc carefully chose the largest and most varicolored of the pearls and handed them to Freawaru, who put them in her pocket after examining and counting them. Then Hoc moved through the hall, accepting the congratulations and good wishes of his men, and giving each of his thanes at least one pearl.

Hildeburh looked at the floor. She had not looked in Finn's face, which he probably interpreted as a sign of modesty or shyness rather than the inertia she felt. He had given her father gems left over from a rape of a goddess. Freyja would not like her to wear pearls.

Hildeburh wished herself back in the garden with Bruna, who talked endlessly about the different ways to prepare and care for the goddess' herbs. In the shadiest corner of the enclosed area grew a plant Bruna had never told her about, just forbidden her to touch. It was long and vine-like, with tiny sharp nettles on the stems and ragged leaves. Last week she had walked over to it and squatted on the ground, eyeing Hildeburh.

"Do you know what this is?" she asked.

"No," said Hildeburh truthfully. "You told me six years ago never to go near it, and I haven't."

"Use the knowledge of the goddess," Bruna said. "Tell me what you can just by looking at it."

Hildeburh looked closely at the plant. "It looks something like the hurrying vine we use to start a late baby coming. It doesn't need a lot of sun but absorbs a lot of water. There is a moldy dust on the leaves. Maybe we could use it for late babies, but I have never seen you harvest it."

Bruna smiled. She had taught her acolyte well, this acolyte she would be losing soon. The goddess' anger did not concern Bruna; she could neither deflect it nor change it; she knew it would come, and if it fell on her, so be it. Bruna knew that the world after death was no palace full of feasting such as Odin's priests described, but a garden of flowers, of continuous birth and life and color and scent.

She had seen it when she drank the teas and tranced into the goddess' world. Bruna was ready for the garden of death if the goddess willed it.

"It would work for late babies but probably be too strong. The contractions would come fast and hard rather than build up, and the tea might not work, the baby come too fast. This vine is called Odin's bane, for it undoes the work of men in making babies. A woman who drinks its tea every day the moon is in the sky will bleed every month in the dark of the moon and bring forth no children. A woman in whom a seed has already latched, and whose bleeding has stopped, can drink the tea and make it start again. It is painful but effective. Do not wash the mold off the leaves. It is part of the magic. While you make the drink, the chant is this:

> *bane of Odin*
> *bring the blood*
> *seed of man*
> *make no child*
> *winter's cold*
> *summer's drought*
> *wolf, raven, eagle:*
> *bring the blood*

Hildeburh had shivered to hear the words but repeated the chant to show she had learned it and carefully added a cutting of Odin's bane to the stock of dried herbs, seeds, and cuttings she would take to Frisia with her.

"Bruna, will the goddess curse me? For leaving you?" Hildeburh finally asked the question that had burned in her all summer.

"I don't know, child. Leaving me is not the issue. Are you leaving Freyja? You are leaving her sworn service but not by your own selfish desires. I have drunk the teas of insight and thought long on your marriage. That it will take place is not a question, unless the sea god sinks Finn's ship when he comes in the autumn. But maybe this marriage will make peace and fruit where there has been death and slaughter and will honor the goddess that way. Take her lore and her teachings to Finn's land, and continue her worship there even as the married Scylding women do here. You are a healer and a birther and will be welcome among your new people."

"And Odin's bane?"

"Take it with you. It is part of Freyja's garden, and you may have need of it there. Perhaps the Frisian women do not know of it. Perhaps you will never use it. But perhaps you will decide," she said brusquely, "that Finn should not father your children."

Finn's hand was under her chin, and he lifted it so he could look into her eyes. "You are daydreaming at your own wedding, my bride," he said gently. "Your father warned me you were a dreamer. My beautiful Danish dream princess. I know you will be happy with me."

Hoc was making his way back to the gift-throne. The next part of the formalities were the queen's, as she was to bear the cup to her husband and the most respected guests, welcoming them. Freawaru poured mead into the chalice she held, one that Hoc had plundered from Jutland years ago. She faced the hall, standing next to the throne, and addressed the gathering.

"Scyldings and Frisians, rejoice in the wedding that joins our tribes. I welcome you all to our hall, to this feast, to the marriage of my only daughter. Our king sits strong on his ancient throne like his father before him, generous to all who come here. Joy and Welcome!" Freawaru passed the cup to Hoc, who drank and handed it back. She passed it to Finn, who also drank, and then to the major thanes of the two lords. Voices broke out in clamor, and slaves began bringing in the feast, setting upon trestle-tables the roasted deer and pig, freshly baked breads, fruit and vegetable jellies, and the last of the fresh harvest. Shellfish stews steamed in decorated pots, and walrus steaks were served with the enormous tusks adorning the platters. Slave girls circulated with pitchers of mead and water and poured drinks into feast cups made from cattle and aurochs horns, banded with precious metals and carved by the warriors during the long winters at home.

Hildeburh and her husband were served after Hoc and Freawaru; Hildeburh's friends and Finn's troop came by their bench in a stream of congratulations and well wishing. When Hildeburh finally turned toward Finn, he was deep in conversation with Hnaef about the pattern welding techniques of the Saxon swordmasters, and he seemed to have forgotten she was there.

All too soon, Freawaru and Sunya and Bruna and the women were around her. They sang the bride-bed song as they escorted Hildeburh, blushing, from the hall:

fruits of harvest
fruits of fall
fruits of marriage
bless them all
bless them, goddess,
bless these two
may their union
be true to you

Hildeburh heard the raucous cheering of the Frisians surrounding Finn as she left the hall.

She and Finn were to spend the night in the queen's burum before their departure the next morning. Earlier in the day Hnaef, now called the Halfhand, had made sure that Hildeburh's dowry and clothes were all securely packed in the eagle-prowed ships that would take her from Scyldingland. Hildeburh started to cry as she let herself realize what she had shut from her mind, that this was the last time she would lie in Freawaru's feather-bed, that tomorrow she would say goodbye, probably for the last time, to her family and people. She remembered the joyous times when she and her friends had brought other brides to bed. When Sunya had married, Hnaef and Hengest had built her burum, and Sunya's friends had made her a loom. The next morning the girls gathered in the burum to tease Sunya, who looked radiantly happy, and exclaim over the necklace of amethysts that Hengest had given her as her morgengabe, the traditional gift of jewelry the groom gave the bride after their first night together.

It was Sunya who took charge. The other women, seeing Hildeburh's tears, were starting to cry as well, and the bride-bed ceremony threatened to become a weepy disaster. "Come on, Hildeburh. This is your wedding night. Don't think about leaving till tomorrow. He's on his way. Let's get you ready."

Sunya and Freawaru dressed her in the night smock that Freawaru had embroidered with flowers of the goddess. Sunya unbraided her hair, and the other women turned down the bed furs and lighted oil lamps. One by one they kissed Hildeburh's cheek and whispered, "May Freyja bless you," and left. Finally Hildeburh was alone with her mother, Bruna, and Sunya.

Bruna sprinkled crushed lilac around the bed, perfuming the room with the scent. She kissed Hildeburh's forehead. "Freyja bless this marriage with fruit and peace. Be true to the goddess, my child, and your life will be strong and happy." Her voice cracked and she left quickly.

Sunya hugged Hildeburh. "You look beautiful. He can't help but love you. I know you will be happy, Hildeburh. You love life too much to live in misery. See you tomorrow."

As Sunya left, Freawaru sat down next to Hildeburh. "He seems a good man, Hildeburh." She thought involuntarily of Finn's visits to the slave quarters, then pushed the image from her mind. "I cannot be happy that you are leaving me, but I can be happy that you will have a good husband." She was silent for a moment as they watched the flame of an oil lamp sputter on its wick. "We have not talked about your future this summer, Hildeburh, and that was a mistake. We have kept silence in the hope that this marriage would not happen and you would not have to leave. I have not taught you queenship because I thought you were a priestess.

"But a priestess wields power much like a queen, and you know this. You have watched me all your life. I have made mistakes, but I have ruled the Scyldings in your father's absences and sometimes even when he is in the hall." She smiled wryly as she thought of the discussions with her husband in her burum. "Make yourself Queen of Frisia as I have done for myself here. You must be first among the women at Folcwalda's hall if you are to be Finn's queen in anything more than name. You have the power of healing. Use it to bind the Frisians to you. If you do not rule, you will be reviled, and I cannot bear to think of it.

"We can say goodbye tomorrow. Sunya is right. Enjoy your wedding night. I hear your husband coming." Freawaru slipped out of the burum.

Hildeburh hadn't thought about using her healing skills as instruments of queenly power, hadn't thought about queenly power at all as she had moved through the summer in her daze, pretending she wouldn't be married in the fall. But here she was, wife to Finn, and someday she would be queen of Friesland. Freawaru had given her much to think about.

Chapter Five

"Hwaet, my Hildeburh," said Finn formally. "I rejoice in the child to be born to us. May it be a prince to continue the line of Folcwalda!" He raised his drinking horn to his father, who raised his in return. They both drank.

Hildeburh sipped at the clear water she kept in the skin bag hanging from her belt. Frisian ways were odd, this announcement of her pregnancy just one instance in which the customs of her husband's people were different from her own. At Hoc's hall, in the late winter and early spring, the men strutted around, noting the swelling bodies of their wives or favorite slave girls, but nothing overt was said among the tribe; the men returned from their summer viking journeys to meet their new offspring. She had told Finn that she was sure the night before; the child would be born in late August. He had immediately told his father and arranged this celebration.

"You must wait until the moon has darkened three times with no blood before you can be sure," her mother and Bruna had told her. Less than a year after their marriage, their first child would be born. An auspicious beginning, Hildeburh admitted to herself. A child with the blood of Danes and Frisians would seal the peace even more firmly, and that was her job in her new home after all.

The Frisians and Danes seemed to have many similarities, including the arrangement of buildings within the frithstowe. Folcwalda had a hall much like Hoc's, where the whole tribe gathered for a feast every three days. Many of the Frisians slept in the hall as well, and the married women had small houses of their own, which the Frisians called cambrai, on the grounds of the hall. The open air kitchen was at the back of the hall, the latrine pit near the slave quarters at the very edge of the compound. Yet there were marked differences. Hildeburh had learned right away that there was no easy intimacy among the cambrai as there was among the Danish burum. A Frisian woman needed her husband's permission to leave the cambrai or its gardens; the Frisian king, she had learned, left two thanes to rule the hall and the women and children when the men went on summer voyages. The queen did not rule.

Indeed there was no queen; Folcwalda's wife had died seven winters before, and it was to her cambrai that Hildeburh had been conducted when she had arrived in Frisia four months previously. Slaves had swept and washed the floor planking; she directed the placement of her dowry chests along the walls and set up her loom herself. Already she was raising ducks to make a featherbed like her mother's.

She looked at Finn, so eager to please his father with a son. Her husband was speaking with some of Folcwalda's thanes; they were planning a hunt for the next day. Finn deftly speared a partridge with his eating knife and put it on the platter they shared. "Eat up, my dear! We want a healthy warrior come summertime!" The men laughed as Hildeburh blushed; she had never heard men talking so openly about babies growing in their mothers' bodies.

Partridges, though, were one thing she definitely liked about her new home. They had been served at her second wedding feast, she remembered, on the night of her arrival in Frisia.

That day was already a blur in Hildeburh's mind. Bleary with seasickness—she had never been on the open ocean—she had been welcomed formally, if briefly, by her father-in-law on the beach. Through the haze of her nausea, Hildeburh noted the tremors in his hands and the greyness of his face; the Lord of the Frisians was not a well man. Finn had gone with his father to the hall, leaving her in the care of a group of women obviously as uncomfortable as she was. When she arrived at her cambrai, she thanked the women, and they immediately left her alone; it was with some relief that she had found a slave waiting inside for her.

"I am Wealh, a gift from your husband, my Lady. I will be attending you here at your cambrai, though on nights when Finn chooses to sleep here I shall sleep with the other slaves. Please feel free to instruct me, my princess. I know our ways are different from yours."

Hildeburh looked at Wealh, a girl not much younger than herself. Wealh was very tall; she would have to duck her head going in and out of the low door of the cambrai. Wealh's other immediately noticeable feature was her enormous feet, splayed on the plank floor with no shoes to hide their size, even in the cold of late autumn. On her left foot, a horned circle quartered by a cross was traced in blue. Hildeburh couldn't help staring.

Wealh grinned, and with that smile Hildeburh realized that she was going to like Wealh. Her mischievous smile was much like Sunya's. "You look at my mark, mistress? I come from the south, a land of warmth and flowers that I hardly remember. When Folcwalda was young, he raided my village, and I was part of his plunder, an overlarge girl child with big feet. But I already had my tattoo, which is what my people call this mark, and thus, when I die, my spirit will be able to find my ancestors in the afterlife. This

is the moon goddess, my Lady, and she watches over me
and all my people."

Talkative slaves were another unusual feature of
Friesland, Hildeburh was to find, but she liked Wealh very
much and took comfort in her presence, especially that
first day. It was Wealh who had found the right clothes
from the dowry chest for the second marriage ceremony;
it was Wealh who had brought her food and drink from
the kitchen, shown her the latrine area, and brought extra
wood for the fire. Together they had made up a bed on a
pallet of fresh straw and covered it with cloth from one of
the chests. Wealh had even taken her to the door of the hall
for the wedding ceremony before Finn's gods.

This feast to celebrate her pregnancy was reminiscent
of her wedding feast, she realized. The men did all the
talking and singing; the women served their husbands
and only occasionally talked among themselves, quietly
in groups of two or three. Her Frisian marriage feast was
much like her Danish one, except she knew only a few
of the hall-sitters, mostly the men who had accompanied
Finn to Scyldingland to collect her. Like the Danes, the
Frisians had dressed in their finest garments and gems
for the wedding feast, with ample jewelry on both the
men's and women's bodies and clothes. The high-roofed
hall was lighted with torches soaked in whale oil, which
gave off a strong, salty smell. She walked the length of
the hall as the bard, a thane of Folcwalda's who (she later

learned) had lost a leg in a raid on the Rhinelanders, sang of the Frisian gods, of Woden and Njord and Tiuw. Hildeburh understood most of the Frisian language—it was so much like her own—and knew that her husband and his followers had had no problems speaking with the Danes. The language of the bard was perhaps older and more formal, because Hildeburh caught only bits of the story, something about brothers hunting with arrows. As she walked, she missed Sunya, needing a woman she knew and trusted to share her second wedding walk but knowing she had to do it alone. She held her head high and tried to look as queenly as possible—she was Hoc's daughter, and a symbol of the peace, wealth, and prestige of the Danes.

"I greet you, new daughter, in the name of Woden All-Father and our gods," said Folcwalda. He sat on his high gift-throne, which was made of wood, rather than stone like Hoc's; carved into its arms were eagles much like those that fronted Frisian ships. Folcwalda's beard of blended white and grey hung below his swordbelt. His blue eyes were sharp, bright, and alert in his aged and wrinkled face though his body seemed small and frail beneath his royal robes. On his head was a broad gold circlet studded with large pearls. His cloak was trimmed with the white fur of the winter weasel; it was old and needed tending. His black tunic, too, was worn and shiny in places, but his swordbelt was thick and supple, made from the finest of elk hide, and studded with more pearls.

He was an imposing figure, despite his age, made more so by the large number of sturdy young thanes that filled his hall. They obviously fought hard for their aging king, for all the Frisians wore gold and silver arm-rings around both of their upper arms, rewards for battle-valor and war-work. Hildeburh realized for the first time why her father had been forced to tear her from service to the goddess and pledge her in peace; the Frisians were a formidable war band, and they looked stronger and more numerous than the Danes.

"You come to us as a pledge of peace between our peoples, a symbol of the union of two glorious tribes." Folcwalda stopped speaking and coughed, a horrid dry sound that echoed in the wooden rafters. He straightened and continued, "I place your hand in the hand of my son to show that Woden's battle lust is sated between our peoples, and that the gifts of Frey will follow, bringing forth children to show the peace in his honor. For Woden is the All-Father, the god of death and battle and knowledge, and Frey is the god of life and growth. May they smile upon this union."

It was a good thing, Hildeburh reflected as she sipped at her water and listened to her husband laugh about tracking elk, that she was not supposed to speak at all during the ceremony, because she had been struck mute with incredulity and then anger at her father-in-law's words. Frey, a male god, was the deity of fruit and growth in Frisia? They had taken Freyja's sacred name and made her into a god?

Later that night, she had asked Finn about Wodin's wife. They were in her bed, his seed trickling down her leg. It was only the second haemod for them, really only the second time they had been alone together, and the second was much like the first. He had come into the cambrai with a horn of mead and dismissed Wealh with a wave of his hand. "Hello, my princess," he had said amiably. "We are now married before my gods as well as yours." He had removed his tunic and breech wrappings and held her face as he kissed her. He tasted of the dark amber mead the Frisians made from honey and grains; his short, dark beard bristled against her cheeks and chin. After she took off her undersmock, he mounted her almost immediately, pushing her thighs apart with his knees and burying his face into her neck. She smelled the cool sea air of the afternoon she had spied on Odin's ceremony, and felt the same nausea and horror that had come from watching the unseeing slave girl in torture and sacrificial death. His hands gripped at her breasts—there would be faint blue marks there later—and after a minute or two of thrusting, he groaned into her ear and was still. She recited in her mind the order for plantings in the western side of the garden. Then he rolled over and wiped his sticky member on the edge of the bed coverings. She breathed deeply once again, not realizing she had been holding her breath.

"What was your childhood like, Finn?" Hildeburh asked in the dark silence.

"Like any other, I suppose. I lived here, with my mother," he said absently.

"And what was she like?"

"My mother? Oh, she was wonderful. I look like her, I think, more than like my father. She was kind and loving. She told me stories and baked honey cakes in that hearth for me. I missed her terribly after my monwart."

"What's that?"

"The Frisian ceremony of manhood. At the autumn ceremony to Woden, when the boy is seven, he puts on the breech wrappings and tunic of a man and lays aside the smock that children wear. Then he hunts and works with the men, especially his father and uncles. He sleeps in the hall, not in his mother's cambrai, and does not see her except on feast days."

"You mean a boy can't see his mother except in the hall after he's seven years old?"

"Yes. Woden All-Father wants our boys to grow into strong warriors, not weaklings clinging to their mothers. The boys need to learn from the men."

"In Scyldingland, the boys have a similar ceremony," said Hildeburh slowly. "But they still see their mothers every day. Women do not go to Odin's rituals, except at midwinter, in Scyldingland. Do they here?"

"No," laughed Finn. "The rites of Woden All-Father are not for women's eyes or ears, even at midwinter. Woden is a god of men's things—power, knowledge, war, death. Women have no place there." His voice softened. "Especially a woman like you, my Hildeburh." He touched her cheek. "I was pleasantly surprised to see how beautiful you are. I know you will be a good wife to me and a good mother to our children. My sword is strong and my boat is swift—I will make sure you need never worry about death or war, Hildeburh."

Or knowledge either, I suppose, thought Hildeburh, although she didn't say it. Instead she said, "Tell me about your gods. Who is Frey?"

"Frey is the god who watches over the land when the men are summer voyaging. He has a huge prick, and he never covers it up—there are lots of stories about that," Finn laughed. "He makes the crops grow and the babies come, spurting his seed through the fields and the women. He does not fight but makes sure that Asgard is prepared to welcome the gods when they return from their wars with giants and trolls. And Tiuw is the god of the sky, and watches that the sun and the moon and the stars and the clouds do their jobs, and Njord is the god of the sea, who provides us with winds and waves for our voyages and fish for our tables..."

"Who is Woden's wife?" Hildeburh asked as Finn paused for breath, forestalling what she saw would be a litany of Frisian gods who governed each segment of their world.

"Woden's wife?" Finn looked at her blankly. "Why would Woden need a wife? All of us, all the gods, all the things of this world are his children that he created with his awesome power. He needs no woman to grow his seed for him.

"But I need you, Hildeburh, and I hope my children from my seed will grow in your womb. Ours is a marriage for tribal peace, but I think we can make it more than that. Can we Hildeburh?"

Impulsively, she threw her arms around his neck and felt her eyes start to fill with tears. All the loneliness and strain of the past four days might be worth it, she thought, if her so-far nondescript husband and she could be happy together. "I would like that very much," was all she said.

"I must sleep in the hall," he said. "But may I come back in the morning?"

Hildeburh was surprised. She had assumed he would come and go as he pleased, as most husbands did in Scyldingland. "Of course, husband. You are always welcome here. Would you...." her voice trailed off as he walked toward the door.

"Yes?" he asked.

"Would you ask your father if I could mend the tunic and cloak he wore tonight, and perhaps make him some new ones? I had planned on weaving you a new cloak this winter, but I can make time for your father's things as well, since there is no queen, and I didn't know if it was custom, and I didn't want to ask him directly, you understand..."

Finn laughed and leaned over to give her a kiss. "Folcwalda will be pleased you noticed, and I will send a slave to you with his formal robes tomorrow. Goodnight, my princess."

That had been the night on which she had begun to like Finn, to think that he was handsome, especially when he laughed, and to hope that he would smile at her and kiss her and call her "my princess" in his oddly formal, yet affectionate way.

The child within her would grow strong and healthy, she would see to that. Hildeburh knew that a boy rather than a girl would make Finn love her more, and seal the peace more firmly. She herself was torn; a girl would be a sign of forgiveness from Freyja. If the goddess blessed her with a daughter, it would show that she was not angry that Hildeburh had left her service. Yet Hildeburh had not left Freyja's worship; she still knew the mysteries, still repeated the prayers. She had not yet been able to assist at a birth or a healing, but she knew that when that time came, she would call on Freyja's power, praying that the goddess' magic would work here as it did in Denmark.

For Hildeburh remembered well the words of her mother: "Use your healing to bind them to you." Freawaru was right; she had to make the Frisians defer to her queenly power, but neither she nor her mother had anticipated that the Frisian women would lead lives so regulated by their men. They participated in only some of the minor religious festivals, most having to do with Njord or Frey, and goddesses were not specifically worshipped by anyone in the tribe. Cyneheard, Folcwalda's bard, had looked at her oddly one night around midwinter when she had requested a song about Frisian goddesses. "Enough stories about Woden and his raven, Cyneheard," she had said in what she thought was a friendly, jesting fashion. "Sing to us of Frisian goddesses. Where are the women in these palaces and battles?"

Cyneheard had looked at her sourly and, after a brief silence, began the story that Finn had told in Hoc's hall about the goddess Neursa who had lost her pearls when Woden raped her.

Wealh had told her later that women weren't supposed to speak out in the hall, just talk quietly among themselves and to their husbands. Hildeburh was still on little more than greeting terms with most of the Frisian women; she had been surprised to hear from Wealh, still her closest confidante, that many men had expressly forbidden their wives to visit her cambrai. "You are a foreigner, my Lady, and your ways are unfamiliar to the Frisians. They do not like a woman who commands the bard, who steps in to mend the king's clothes as if she were the queen, who talks of healing and goddesses and demands to know why there are none here."

"I don't demand..." Hildeburh began.

"Just by asking, my Lady, you seem to demand, because no one has ever asked before. You are the highest ranking woman in Frisia, but you still rank below the lowest boy who has gone through monwart."

"So I am little better than a slave," Hildeburh said morosely.

"You are much better off," said Wealh pertly. "You need lay with only one of the Frisian men, and Finn would kill any of the others who tried to touch you."

Hildeburh's face burned a deep red, and she thought for the first time of the humiliation the female slaves must face, having to be always available for haemod whenever any of the men felt like it. She remembered the way Bjorn's hands had felt, five years before, under her smock, stroking her nipples until they ached with the longing she felt, and she knew she would never feel that with Finn, but at least there was a sense of amiability between them. Wealh couldn't expect even that.

"I'm sorry, Wealh. I spoke without thinking."

"It's fine, mistress. They don't choose me very often anyway, with my big feet and tall frame. Lots of these men like to cover their women, not find their beards at her ribcage."

The women laughed, and the tension dissipated. "You must help me, Wealh. I cannot live the rest of my life shut up in this cambrai and going to feasts where nobody talks to me. At home, I served the goddess Freyja who watched over women in chidlbirth and all those in need of healing. That is my calling, Wealh; I am a birther and a healer, and I wish to continue doing those things here in my new home."

"Have you told Finn this?"

"No, not yet. I wanted to see what things were like here, and I thought I would just befriend your healers and birthers and begin to help them, but there aren't any, or I'm not allowed to talk to them, or something—who delivers the babies around here? Who will attend me next summer? You? You and me by ourselves?"

Wealh's face lighted up. "Mistress, so soon?"

"Don't tell anyone. I shouldn't even have told you. I'm not sure yet. I've missed only two moons of bleeding. But honestly, what will happen? Who will help me?"

"The slaves help each other, and the mother and sisters of the mother-to-be help the Frisians. I don't know what your case is, my Lady. You are the only foreigner here who is not a slave. Finn has no female relatives."

In Denmark, that would mean that Hildeburh would pass the cup at the feast, to greet the king and his most honored retainers. But she had seen no passing of the cup, even at this feast to celebrate the expected child of the prince, and she idly wondered if she would ever be queen enough in Frisia to use the formal speech and praise her husband to his assembled company in the way that Freawaru did.

A few weeks before, she had asked Finn to recommend some of the older Frisian women, of his father's generation, that she could ask for advice, and gently suggested that he talk to their husbands before she invited them to her cambrai.

Finn seemed surprised. "Modthryth and Cynethryth will certainly wait upon you," he said.

"Husband, Wealh tells me that some of the women have been forbidden by their husbands to visit with the foreigner—meaning me. I would not want to embarrass you or myself by speaking to a woman who is not supposed to speak to me."

"So that's it," Finn said thoughtfully. "I had wondered why you were not getting to know the other women. I just thought it was your natural shyness and a new place. Well," he frowned, "this is ridiculous. Speak to Modthryth and Cynethryth, but also know that the wives of some of my companions will be speaking to you as well." He left the cambrai with a dark look on his face.

So it had happened that the week before this feast celebrating her pregnancy, Hildeburh had found herself making tea and discussing her loom with two women somewhat older than her mother. They had dressed for the occasion, with jewelry and robes almost as formal as those Hildeburh had seen the night of her wedding feast. She had trouble telling them apart and discovered in the course of the conversation that they were sisters, married to thanes of Folcwalda long before he had become king.

"And you have children?" she asked politely when they had finished examining her loom, over which stretched a new cloak for Finn, dark blue with streaks of yellow running over the shoulders.

"Oh yes," Cynethryth answered. Her swollen hands held the cup of tea, and through the wrinkles and brown spots, Hildeburh could see the enlarged knuckles of a severe form of the ache that came with the rain, twisted fingers and tightened hips and knees. She had a herb preparation in her dowry chest that could reduce the swelling immediately, if temporarily, but knew better than to mention it. "We each have three sons, all about Finn's age, and I have two daughters as well."

"And who," Hildeburh leaned forward, "this is very awkward, and I hope you won't be offended, but who helps the babies come into the world? Did you assist each other? And is there a woman with more knowledge than the others, who in Denmark we would call a birther? I ask only because, if the prince and I are lucky enough to conceive a child this winter, I need to know who will assist at the birth. I don't want to offend the customs of my new people, you see, and I didn't know whom to ask."

The two old women looked puzzled, but they both smiled at her. "In Frisia, we have no birther, as you call it. The mothers and sisters of the woman assist her when her time comes. Birth, after all, is in the hands of Frey. We do what we can for her, but he determines if the birth is healthy and whether the mother and child live. It is a sad truth, princess, that the god has not been kind to us in recent years. The north hillside is full of the ashes of new mothers and newborn babies. We have found that if a woman can have one, she can have many, but many women die with their first one," Cynethryth said.

"Gefean is angry with us," Modthryth said abruptly.

Cynethryth wheeled about. "Hush up. We'll have none of that talk before the princess."

"Who is Gefean?" Hildeburh asked.

"It is nothing, princess, just an old superstition. I don't know who will attend you this summer," she rushed on, "should such a happy event occur. You and Finn both have no female relations."

Modthryth broke in, "But I think no one would think it wrong if we volunteered. We will help you. I am glad you have come, my Lady. Frisia needs a queen."

Cynethryth rose, pulling her sister up with her. "Of course we would be happy to help, princess. Please don't think my sister is imposing. But we have taken enough of your time. We must bid you goodbye."

Hildeburh watched as they walked past her gardens where she was cultivating Freyja's herbs as well as carrots and greens. She wondered if all visits between women here were so formal that they seemed like visits between tribes. Hildeburh thought neighbors should be on easier and more intimate terms. Cynethryth and Modthryth passed by the little duck house she and Wealh had built and went around the corner of another cambrai, out of sight.

I didn't even get to ask about healing sickness and war wounds, she thought to herself, *and I now have two elderly birth attendants who probably know less than I do.* But some of the women obviously were happy she had arrived, even if they hadn't said so. And who was Gefean? She had sensed that asking Finn might not be prudent, and she had gone to her loom to think.

Finn was wearing that cloak now, and it made his short body look more statuesque, as she had intended. Folcwalda, too, looked more majestic if still not robust; she had cleaned and repaired the ermine trim on his cloak and woven him a new black tunic of fine wool. His old tunic was in her scrap bag where it belonged—Hildeburh had found it hard to believe a king's raiment could become so bedraggled.

She surveyed the company with pleasure. Recently, the men had been making noises about getting the boats out of winter storage and making them ready for the summer season, which began when the ice in the harbor fully broke up. Hildeburh was feeling more at ease among the Frisians; Cynethryth spoke to her frequently at feasts; other women were beginning to offer smiles and welcomes; her husband obviously favored her; and she was pregnant. In addition, she knew she could begin her work after the men left; Finn had promised her the night before in the glow of the news of her pregnancy.

"Husband, Cynethryth told me that many women here die in childbed. I know I could be of some help. Bruna taught me much before I left Scyldingland, and I have assisted at many, many births."

Finn looked at the floor, uncomfortable discussing things that happened among women when the men were gone. "That is Frey's work, not ours. We must accept what the god ordains. It is true that many warriors leave on their summer voyages with the fear that they will return to find their wives' ashes buried on the north hill. But Frey takes life as well as gives it. He must have his reasons."

"Finn," she said carefully, having planned her speech with a lot of thought, "if I could help half the women who might die, and half of them have boys, that is three or four more warriors for your band every year. When you are king, you will have more strong, young followers if you order the women to let me help them when their time comes. My birthing skills are at your service, my lord. It seems to me that I should use what powers I have to assist you in your kingship."

After a pause, Finn said, "I pray to Woden that Folcwalda will live to great age, but I am already taking on some of his duties. He still commands his eagle ship, but I train the younger men and make the boats ready for the season. I, not he, lead the beach charges in the raids. I know that within a few summers he will remain on the sea with the other old men, drinking and singing as they wait for the return of the fighters from the landings."

Hildeburh had always wondered how the old men managed to comport themselves during battles that seemed to require speed, strength, and agility; she stored the information about the old men waiting in a ship offshore to think about it later.

Finn continued, "You are right, my princess. I will be king soon, in all but name, and I will need more warriors if our neighbors are to continue to regard the Frisians with awe. I will speak of it at the feast tomorrow, and come summer you will be a birther for our tribe as you were for yours." Then his face darkened. "But such birthing must not interfere with our gods, Hildeburh. Assist at births, and respect Frey as you do it. You will be birthing warriors for Woden, and the Scylding goddess you have sometimes spoken of has no place in our world."

She had assented, thinking that Freyja was present at birthing time whether Finn liked it or not, and spent the next day weeding Freyja's garden, mentally counting the number of women who might give birth that summer, planting extra stalks of the plants to make Freyja's tea, and pruning the small vine of Odin's bane that grew in a shady corner.

Finn's voice ended her reverie. He was standing and the gathered company was looking at him expectantly. He raised his drinking horn. "My King and my people, we rejoice today in the lengthening of our royal line through another generation. To honor this unborn child, I wish to give my princess a mark of my favor, as her husband, lord, prince, and king to be." He removed from a leather pouch on the trestle table before him a shining circlet, thinner than his own but just as rich. It had been forged of thick gold with four enormous rubies in the front. Each of the rubies was surrounded by small pearls, all pure white, and the gold itself was worked into an interlaced design that alternately looked like interlocking monsters or entangled vines. Hildeburh looked at it in wonder, yearning to touch it. She had never dreamed of owning anything so precious or so beautiful.

As Finn placed it on her head, he said, "This circlet belonged to my mother; it is the mark of the Frisian queen. I know that Hildeburh will be a gracious queen, just as Aelfgyth before her was, and she will bring honor to this circlet as my mother did. With a change of queens come other changes, and I will tell you one of them now."

There was some shifting and muttering among the assembled people; Cyneheard spat audibly into the straw at the edges of the hall. Change, especially that obviously instigated by the foreigner, was not welcome. "Hildeburh is a skilled birther, the term the Scyldings use for a woman whose knowledge makes her the one to attend the births of the babies born in the summer when the men are making viking journeys. My princess has told me she thinks she can help us so that there will be fewer deaths each summer. And fewer deaths now," Finn could see disagreement, refusal, and argument on many faces in the hall and he raised his voice to dominate the gathering, "means more strong warriors later to serve our king! A birther will not deny the gods their rights but help us to serve Woden better, with a bigger troop of armored warriors whirling swords for the glory of Folcwalda and Frisia and Woden. This will be done!"

The group of Finn's closest followers, Handschue and Aescher and Edgheard and some others, immediately started cheering and howling their approval of their prince. Others joined in, and when Finn saw that most of the group was with him, he sat down.

"Alfgyth's circlet becomes you, princess," he said kindly. "For both our sakes, I hope that there are many healthy babies waiting on the beach next fall when the eagle ships come home."

"Yours will be among them, my lord," she said firmly. "Thank you for the circlet. It is a kingly gift and one I did not expect."

"I hadn't planned on giving it to you until after our first boy was born," he smiled, "but that plan was made before we met."

A woman Hildeburh had nodded at from a distance made her way through the hall to Hildeburh and Finn's place. "My Lady, I am Frigga, wife to Handschue, thane of your husband, our prince. I have not spoken with you before," she blushed and looked down, "but I would be honored if you would come to my cambrai tomorrow."

"Of course, Frigga," Hildeburh smiled. Finn had obviously made his wishes known among his men, as he had said he would. "I am honored to be asked," she said formally.

"And princess, I had no idea you were a birther. Handschue and I expect our first child this summer, and I am afraid for myself and my baby. I have been ill, princess, not eating, and I fear the baby is not growing. Oh, I should wait, and tell you this later, I am sorry, princess."

"No, no," Hildeburh said. She took Frigga's arm and motioned for her to sit next to her. "I am a birther, and I would like to help you and your husband, of whom Finn has spoken so highly. How long have you been married?"

"We married two autumns ago, but no child started that first winter. Sometimes I thought my bleeding had stopped, but I would miss only a moon and then it would start again, heavier and worse than before, with a lot of pain.

Hildeburh nodded, and before she could reply two more women stood in front of her. "Princess, I am Astart, and this is Lyda; we too are wives of your husband's thanes, and expect babies this summer."

Soon Hildeburh felt more at home than she had since her arrival in Frisia, sitting in a hall with a group of women her age, discussing their children and the months ahead. Astart had a baby boy who could walk, and Lyda had two girls already. Hidleburh knew from watching the Scylding women how hard it was for a pregnant woman to take care of herself properly when she had other small ones in the burum to take care of as well. They were laughing about Lyda's enormous desire for honeycakes during this and her other pregnancies when Cyneheard's voice shook the hall.

"This is an abomination, my King! These women sit by your royal high table, by your gift-throne talking of things that belong in the cambrai, not in the hall! The hall is the place of songs of battle, of men who sleep with their swords at their sides to serve their king at any hour of the day or night. Go!" He came toward them, his blue eyes furious in his time-ravaged face, hobbling on the crutch he used where his right leg had been. He stopped and leaned on one of the trestles, brandishing the crutch as if it were the sword he had been forced to put away years before.

"Go! Do not profane this hall, this feast of Woden All-Father, with your women's talk!"

Frigga, Astart, and Lyda immediately jumped up and scurried back to their husbands. Hildeburh remained seated and looked at Finn. She knew if she stood up, acknowledged Cyneheard's command, that she would never be queen in Frisia. She meant to establish at this moment that no man could command her except the king or her husband. She glared at Cyneheard from under the gleaming circlet and said nothing. Silence echoed in the hall even more fully than the happy chatter that had preceded it.

Folcwalda stood. "Cyneheard," he said in a voice still rich if somewhat muted from the kingly tones it must once have possessed, "this outburst is an affront to the Lady of Frisia, who is not a guest but a member of our tribe, having pledged peace between ourselves and the Danes. You cannot order people to leave my hall, though if you do not like this company, you may absent yourself until such time as I require your presence here. An insult to the princess is an insult to her husband, my son, and thus to me."

"My lord," said Cyneheard quietly, "you know I would never wish to insult you. To honor you is my only desire."

"Yes, I know that, my loyal thane. You have lost a leg for me, and you still serve me well with songs and counsel. I am fortunate to have a companion such as yourself."

The king rose. "I will retire now. Goodnight to all," he said quietly. Cyneheard glared at Hildeburh as Folcwalda slowly made his way through the hall to the king's chamber on the east side. His slaves would be waiting there to attend to him.

Hildeburh let her breath out slowly. The flow of power in the hall confused and exhilarated her at the same time. The circlet weighed on her forehead; she looked forward to taking it off and examining its workmanship.

As Folcwalda reached the door to his chamber, Hildeburh saw him clutch at his left side and double over. Women's shrieks rose above the general noise of the hall as the gathered company fervently discussed Finn's gift and announcement and Cyneheard's outburst. Without thinking, Hildeburh left her seat by the high table and rushed to her father-in-law's side.

Hildeburh would have liked to have screamed too; Folcwalda was vomiting blood in streams. He lay on his side in the shadows of the torchlight, surrounded by the hall clutter of benches and trestles, his body jerking and twisting as he retched again and again. Blood ran out of his nose as well, and with her healer's eye Hildeburh noted instantly that while some of the blood was dark, almost black, and somewhat congealed, some was bright red and fresh.

"Don't just stand there," she snapped at the terrified slaves who were peering at the scene from the chamber door. "Help me get your master to his bed." Two dark, smooth-skinned men lifted Folcwalda and carried him into his chamber.

Hildeburh pushed inside behind Finn and Cyneheard and some others. The king's chamber was a sacred space; deer antlers hung over his bed, covered with an enormous bearskin, a trophy from a long ago hunt. The wealth of the Frisians lay in chests and boxes stacked along the walls; two of the slaves of the king were always awake and present to guard it. On the wall opposite the bed was a shrine to Odin, a one-eyed raven painted above a small table stained with the blood of animal sacrifices. Small braziers heated the room; their smoke vented through horizontal slits in the roof.

Hildeburh made her way to Folcwalda, who was lying semiconscious on top of the bearskin. A slave wiped the blood from Folcwalda's clothes and beard; the king groaned and spat more blood. She lifted his tunic, exposing his abdomen.

Folcwalda's slaves immediately tried to restrain her. "No one may touch the royal person without his permission, mistress. The king's body is sacred."

Hildeburh looked at the slave with contempt. She was glad she had left the crown on her head. "You may assist me while I examine the king. If he is displeased with my conduct after he recovers, he may deal with it as he pleases."

Folcwalda's trunk was swollen with patches of red under the rib cage and in the groin area. As the slaves busied themselves in emptying the chamber of curious onlookers, Hildeburh started palpating the abdomen, concentrating in the sections where the redness and swelling were most obvious. Finn stood slightly behind her, watching.

"Did you know your father was sick, Finn?" she asked.

"I knew he wasn't as healthy as he had been in the past. He has been coughing a lot, and complaining about having trouble sleeping. He hasn't been nearly as strong as he used to be—but I didn't think he was this ill."

"Then Folcwalda has been kingly even in his illness," Hildeburh proclaimed, looking specifically at Cyneheard, who had not left the room. "He is very ill and probably has been for a long time. Feel here," she directed to her husband and guided his hands to the lower left area of Folcwalda's abdomen. "Do you feel those lumps?"

"They feel like rocks or pebbles," he said.

"They are a type of growth, an illness caused by evil spirits in the bodies of otherwise healthy people. Sometimes women get them in their breasts, even when they are young; in men, if they get them, they usually grow in this area as they age. Folcwalda has been in a lot of pain for at least half a year, probably more. The lumps grow bigger and press upon other organs in the body so that they do not work correctly." She looked at the slaves, "Has the king been having trouble relieving himself? And has he been vomiting in the morning?"

When the slaves nodded, she said to her husband, "The lumps are eating away at the parts of his body that control and process the food he eats. At some point, they will weaken his system thoroughly enough that he will die. The disease is much progressed; he does not have long to live. I am sorry to have to tell you this, husband."

Finn fell to his knees at the edge of his father's bed. "Father!" he cried in a voice of anguish as he grasped Folcwalda's hand.

At his son's cry, Folcwalda half-opened his eyes. Hildeburh was astounded; she had not told Finn, but she had been sure Folcwalda would never regain consciousness. He spoke in a low, creaky voice that she could hardly hear.

"Valhalla calls me, my son. Woden needs me now." More blood dripped from the side of his mouth as he spoke. Finn tenderly wiped it away with the edge of his cloak. "I know you will be a good king for my people, Finn. If the child is a boy, name him Raefn, for he will have the knowledge of Woden's raven and the black hair of your princess, who will be a birther for us with my blessing."

Well, that settles that, Hildeburh thought grimly as she watched Folcwalda's life slip away. She felt grief not for Folcwalda, whom she didn't really know, but for her husband, who had idolized his father and would miss him dearly.

It seemed like time stopped in the king's chamber. As the torches burned down, the slaves slipped through the shadows attending to the dying king's last needs, and no one in the room spoke. The only sound was the king's labored breathing. Hildeburh could feel Cyneheard's eyes burning into her back, but she remained at Finn's side, establishing herself as her husband's companion. She knew Cyneheard wanted to tell her to go but didn't dare. Through the thick oak doors she could hear movement in the hall as the Frisians waited for news of their king. Although the night was almost over, no one had left the hall.

Finally, as the grey light started to lift over the eastern forest, Folcwalda moaned, and Hildeburh heard the death rattle as he breathed his last. She whispered to herself:

> *Take him, goddess, to the garden*
> *Take him where the flowers grow*
> *Take him where the sun will shine*
> *Take him where Freyja's peace will go*

Finn rose from the side of the bed where he had knelt all night and closed his father's eyes. He faced the thanes in the room.

"Folcwalda has been called to Woden." His eyes sagged at the corners from the sleeplessness of the deathwatch. Then he strode through the door to tell the assembled tribe that their king had died.

Cyneheard snatched at her arm as she followed Finn. "I saw you muttering your witch words over our king's body," he began.

Hildeburh wrenched her elbow from his grasp. "I sorrow in the death of my father-in-law," she said formally, "and now I must attend my husband." She swept past him into the hall.

Finn was standing before the eagle throne, looking at his thanes around him. Handschue lifted his drinking horn. "Folcwalda goes to Valhalla!" he shouted. "And Finn is king of Friesland! Finn! Finn!"

The others took up the chant until the hall shook with the shouted repetition of Finn's name, and amid the noise of cheering and weeping, Finn looked across the wide room at Hildeburh, still wearing her ruby-studded circlet, met her eyes, and raised his horn to her before holding his arm out in a gesture for her to join him on the dais.

Chapter Six

"The feast is arranged, Finn, and I will be there to pass the cup. Lyda is resting; the baby will probably not come for some more hours." Lyda had wanted to give birth before the men's autumn return, but Hildeburh had known all summer that since Lyda had last bled just after the midwinter festival, she would have her baby in the fall. The queen turned toward the fire. "Raefn, no—fire is hot! It burns little boys' hands. Come over here." Hildeburh led the chubby two year old to a low chest against a wall far from the hearth. She helped Raefn lift the lid, and he squealed with delight when he saw the old wooden cups and spindles there. He picked out two cups and started banging them together.

Finn reclined on their featherbed, watching Raefn. "This winter I'll make him a tiny sword and shield, and carve him a helmet so he can start to play with the other boys. He's big, isn't he? He's bigger than Handschue's boy, and Brecc is older than Raefn by a few months, right?"

"Well, children grow differently, husband. But Raefn and Brecc are both strong and healthy. There is no disease in Frisia this fall, so the winter should be an easy one for the children. We'll have some runny noses, but I pray no fevers."

He grasped her hand and pulled her down next to him. "We are stronger and healthier because you are here, my princess." Raefn looked at his parents, pulled himself upright, and toddled over to the bed. "Fa-fa, ma-ma, Raef," he said, and his dark eyes lighted with pleasure as Finn picked him up and snuggled him between his father and mother. Finn and Hildeburh dozed as Raefn sang them a nonsense song.

"I must check on Lyda," Hildeburh said reluctantly.

"Raef go, too!" her son demanded imperiously.

"Yes, you may visit too, little prince. Let's find our cloaks. Winter is coming."

Finn rose as well. "I'll meet you later in the hall," he said. "I told Edgtheow and his men that we'd all go hunting this afternoon. Maybe get some aurochs. We could use the horn as well as the meat."

Finn's hall was still the center of the Frisian world, though the king's chamber was rarely used. Most nights he slept in the queen's cambrai. In the three summers he had been king, the treasure stored around Woden's shrine and under the deer antlers in the chamber had almost doubled; Finn had ventured down rivers to Helvitia and across the western sea to Bretonland in his successful voyaging. His people called his frithstowe Finnsburgh to honor their king and his growing power. Tribes had begun to send emissaries to Finnsburgh with tribute to make treaties with Frisia and avoid a clash with Finn and his warriors in their eagle-prowed ships. This morning a group of Jutes had come on just such a mission.

Hildeburh and Raefn made their way through the compound along the paths that the women had lined with the trunks of young trees the previous summer. Hildeburh had planned and supervised the project, and had assigned groups of older children to fill the walkways with rocks for drainage. Now the Frisians could walk among the cambrai and to the hall and not worry about mud.

Many women were in their gardens, turning over the earth for its winter rest, harvesting the last of the turnips, or planting bulbs along the borders near the fences. Hildeburh greeted each by name, often stopping to inquire about children or a healing injury. When they arrived at Lyda's cambrai, she sent Raefn into the garden to dig for turnips with a blunt stick. Lyda and Aescher's other children were already there under the watchful eye of a Breton slave that Aescher had brought back from last summer's raids to help Lyda care for their growing family.

Hildeburh entered the cambrai. Aescher had put planking over the hard dirt floor two winters before, and Hildeburh slipped off her light boots to keep the room as clean as possible. Lyda was walking around the room, her hands supporting her enormous belly.

"You look wonderful, Lyda. This will be another easy one," Hildeburh said lightly.

Lyda grimaced, then laughed. "They only seem easy afterwards, my Queen. This one is taking its own slow time." Suddenly her face whitened, and she reached for a smooth cylinder of ebony, the hardest wood that grew in the Frisian forests. She put it in her mouth and bit down, leaning against the edge of one of her dowry chests as the wave of the contraction passed over her. The wood helped her change her screams of pain into muffled groans.

"That was a long one," Hildeburh observed. "This baby may come sooner than we thought. Let me check you again."

This was the part of her birthing work that the Frisian women, even those who liked and trusted her, had viewed with the most suspicion. The hands of a woman entering Frey's sacred space seemed sacrilegious to the Frisians, and it was only Hildeburh's queenly insistence that made them acquiesce. Respecting their unease, Hildeburh did not check them as frequently as Bruna and she had checked the Danish women.

Lyda lay down on her bed, a pallet of straw covered with weavings, and Hildeburh went over to the fire. She turned her body to block her actions from the women gathered in the cambrai; there were widespread rumors about the magic she commanded. She stared at the glow of the embers dancing at the edges of the fire, yellow and red and orange outlining the crags and edges of the logs, until she saw the fire and then the sun of Freyja's garden, made her way to the hot spring in the woods, and plunged her hands to purify them for the goddess' work. She heard a noise among the trees that ringed the spring and looked up to find a white elk gazing at her with gentle, knowing eyes.

"You are mine, Queen Hildeburh, and do my work. And the girl is mine, too. Remember that. Lyda's daughter Elena is mine, too." Hildeburh's vision cleared, and she stood before Lyda's fire in the chill of a Frisian autumn.

She turned to the bed and gently pressed her left hand against Lyda's abdomen, making sure that the baby was still head down. It had dropped more steeply since morning, and as Hildeburh probed Lyda's birth canal with her right hand, she realized it was almost wide enough to let the baby through.

"Just a bit longer, Lyda. You'll be nursing your dau-, your baby, before the feast begins." Hildeburh cursed herself inwardly for her slip as Lyda's sisters exchanged glances. No use giving Cyneheard more reason to call her a witch.

Hildeburh returned to the fire and removed a leather pouch of herbs from her pocket. She still made her dresses in the Scylding fashion, finding that with a two-year-old son she had even more need of the pocket than before. Last spring, she had noticed some of the other women were copying the queen's fashion, and many Frisian women now used pockets rather than bulky baskets for spindles and for their children's cups and snacks.

Hildeburh made an infusion of Freyja's tea in one of Lyda's larger jars, murmuring the words of the prayer under her breath. To the gathered women—Lyda, her mother, and her two sisters—it sounded like the queen was humming tunelessly. Hildeburh placed the jar on a chest next to Lyda's bed. "Drink half of this now and half when the sun has gone below the roof edge of Finn's hall." Lyda was up and walking again, stopping during contractions, and as she walked she sipped at the tea. Hildeburh dipped the blade of her knife in the boiling water and placed it carefully at the side of the dowry chest next to two lengths of strong wool thread.

Three summers before, the women of the Frisians did not believe it—the queen could make a drink that took away most of the pain of birth. Lyda had been among the first, and she eagerly told the others—Frigga, Astart, all the expectant women—how much easier it was with the queen's magic.

"This is it, Hildeburh. I know the feeling. I think I'm ready."

Hildeburh crossed the room back to the bed and gestured for Lyda to lie down again. Another probe revealed that Lyda was right; the baby's head was on the way through the widened birth canal. "Put the cloths down," she said crisply to the other women, and she helped Lyda stand and make her way to the center of the room where her mother was spreading a broad, clean cloth of soft woven wool.

Hildeburh smiled at the others, women she didn't know as well as Lyda. "We've done this together once before, so we know what to do. You hold her arms—Thorgilda on the left and Gisela on the right, it was lucky last time. Ludhild, be ready with the wrappings; you'll hold the baby while I cut the cord and keep her warm afterwards." *No use pretending anymore that I don't know it's a girl*, she thought.

"Okay, we'll do two pushes, then a break for a walk, then two more, then a walk. We'll see how we're doing after that." Lyda nodded as another contraction began. "Use it—push! Bear down!" she cried.

Lyda squatted on the cloth, her sisters holding her arms as she strained through the contraction, which felt to her like a mild cramp because of the tea. Her cheeks flushed red; her hands shook; and sweat dripped down the middle of her back. Between contractions, her mother helped her drink some more of the now-cooled tea.

"Even if the baby comes quickly, the effects will help with the afterbirth and the beginning of your body's healing," Hildeburh said gently to Lyda. She wanted to remind her that the end was in sight, that the pain and labor would end soon.

The next contraction began, and Lyda pushed more, and her whole face turned bright red. When it was over, she walked about the room, breathing heavily, her bare feet slapping on the planking, now soiled with blood and womb water. Slaves would clean it later that night.

The women repeated the process, two more long pushes and another walk, and then Hildeburh checked the baby's position. "We're very close," she said excitedly. "Less than five more, and the baby's here. I can almost see the head."

Lyda resumed her position as she bore down again. She bellowed out a cry of surprise and joy as she felt the baby slip from her body. Hildeburh deftly caught the infant, cradling the head in the palm of her left hand while her right hand held the tiny buttocks, and in one smooth flow of motion she handed the baby to Ludhild, tied two knots in the cord with the threads, swung around to get her knife, and cut the cord between the knots, three fingers' width from the child's body. Then she slapped the baby girl on the soles of her tiny feet. When the baby obligingly howled in protest, Hildeburh turned back to Lyda. Ludhild could take care of Elena.

Elena was, indeed, the name chosen by Aescher as he named his daughter in front of his king before the start of the feast that evening. Elena's deep baby eyes reflected the torchlight as she gazed at her dark-bearded father in her first, brief period of newborn alertness. Ludhild bowed her head to her son-in-law to signal her daughter's gratitude for his acceptance of the child and then bore the baby Elena back to Lyda's cambrai.

Hildeburh had left Thorgilda and Gisela tending to Lyda; there was no snow left from the previous winter, so Hildeburh had left the sisters detailed instructions and herbs for reducing swelling. Lyda would both drink tea made from the herbs and apply the herbs' poultices directly to the birth area. "Let her walk around if she wants," Hildeburh had instructed, "but nothing more than around the cambrai, and DON'T let the children come in." Then she had gone back to her quarters to dress for the feast, slipping into the hall just as the warriors returned from the hunt.

After the naming ceremony, the feast celebrating the Jutes' mission began. Hildeburh stood at the side of the eagle-armed gift throne, holding a chalice and surveying the assembled company. Historically, the Jutes were the enemies of her people, the Danes. Sometimes her longing for Scyldingland swept over her like a wave, and she found herself breathing hard and clenching her hands to keep herself from crying as she thought about her mother and Bruna and Sunya and Hoc's frithstowe. When Finn was sullen or raging, Hildeburh would curse herself for not marrying Bjorn, for her father could not have pledged her in peace had she already been married.

The Jutish slaves in Denmark had seemed a rough, unmannered group. Their clothes were simple, their leatherwork poor. Hoc raided Jutland for slaves and for livestock; they had no craftsmen who could work metal or leather or bone into fine objects. Hoc was proud that there were no Danish slaves in Jutland. He had kept the Jutes subdued and fearful during his reign.

They were fearful of Frisia now, too, it seemed, and Hildeburh recognized the dark, wiry look of the Jutes among those mingled with the Frisians in the hall. Their leader Edgtheow stood before the gift-throne. Two of his men had placed a large, plain chest behind him; Hildeburh assumed it contained a portion of the tribute the Jutes had brought to appease her husband. The thirty head of cattle she had already seen, and ordered driven to the sequence of forest clearings where the Frisians grazed their livestock.

She could see Finn at the side of her vision; he sat on his throne, his hands resting lightly on the eagle heads. He looked splendid, his short tunic revealing the muscles in his massively strong legs, his pearl studded circlet glinting and shining. A fine bronze collar adorned his neck; he wore an ornamented swordbelt with a dark green leather scabbard.

He turned to her. "My queen," he said formally, "today we greet Edgtheow and his Jutish band, who come in peace to Frisia."

She raised the cup slightly above her head. "Welcome, Jutes, to the hall of Finn, King of Frisia, and warrior of the northern and western seas. Our great king keeps this land in peace and plenty and with this pledge I welcome you to Frisia. Drink with us in peace." She passed the cup to Finn, who saluted Edgtheow in welcome before he drank and handed it back to her. She stepped from the dais and passed the cup to Edgtheow, then to the five other Jutes who had accompanied him and to five of her husband's men. When she returned to her place next to the gift-throne, slaves entered with pitchers of mead and began filling the horns and cups of the rest of the assembled company.

"Finn, son of Folcwalda, King of Friesland, and warrior of the northern and western seas," Edgtheow began. "We come in peace and seek to be your allies, not your enemies, and we wish to join you in your conquests rather than have the wrath of your swords turned against us. To that end, we have brought gifts to show our goodwill. You have already seen the sleek cattle that came in our holds to thicken your herds and add new blood. In addition, I bring you these gifts." He stepped aside and lifted the lid of the chest. Within it were swords and battle axes, plain but strongly made, a golden torque, and a leather pouch of amethysts.

"Edgtheow, your words and gifts and deeds are noble," Finn answered. "You are welcome as an ally." He stood and crossed to the treasure chest. "These gifts and your fighting strength enrich my warband." He removed the torque from the chest and handed it to Edgtheow, saying, "Keep this torque as a symbol of our alliance, my first gift to you for your good service in joining my company." He bent over, picked up the amethysts, and gestured to his slaves to remove the rest of the treasure to the king's chamber.

"Aescher, two amethysts for you, one for your new little daughter whose beauty will grace this hall in years to come. Cyneheard, a stone for your songs and wise counsel for me and for my father when he was alive. Handschue, an amethyst for your war-work of the past summer, for though you were already rewarded, nothing could truly suffice, and thus I give you more treasure to show my ever growing regard for your prowess and skill."

Hildeburh watched as her husband worked his way around the hall, giving treasure and acclaim and binding his men to him. She knew and approved the reasons for his actions; he was establishing Edgtheow as a follower, not an ally king, and one whom Finn could command. Edgtheow might be king of the Jutes, but in Finn's eyes, he was not an equal.

Now Finn was allied to the Danes, through her, and to the Jutes as well. She watched as Finn and Edgtheow sat down together, recalling the day's hunt, and wondered what this new alliance would mean for her people. Finn was strong enough to bend both his allies to his will and keep them from fighting one another.

She noticed the aging Modthryth alone at the lower end of the hall. Her sister Cynethryth had died the previous winter, refusing to the last Freyja's comfort. Hildeburh had not been able to catch Modthryth when she was alone and lucid enough to answer inquiries about her mysterious references to something called Gefean during their very first meeting three years before, though Hildeburh had wondered about it occasionally. Modthryth, now a widow as well, roamed the frithstowe muttering to herself and inadvertently scaring the young children, who all thought she was a witch. Hildeburh crossed the hall to greet her.

"Good even, Modthryth," Hildeburh said, "may I join you?"

"Oh yes, my Lady, do take some ease with me and let the kings talk their war talk. How does the prince?"

"He grows, and eats, and causes no end of trouble," Hildeburh laughed. "Most nights I am worn out from chasing him."

"My Lady is a good mother, an example to the people. And we do not bury mothers under the north hill now that you are here. Frey is no longer angry with Folcwalda's people." She cast a sly glance at Hildeburh.

"Modthryth, I have been longing to ask you since we first met—who or what is Gefean? Your sister walks in shadows and cannot tell you to hush."

"I have been waiting for you to ask, Queen. My sister hated me because I knew the story as well as she did, and she feared the wrath of her husband should it ever be known. Cynethryth spent her life trying to keep her husband happy so he would not beat her, Lady. The idea of a woman having power was strange and frightening for her."

"But what of Gefean, Modthryth? What is the story that Cynethryth didn't want you to tell?"

"Gefean cursed our land when Folcwalda's father's grandfather came and profaned her sacred grove. He forced haemod upon her blue-handed priestesses, our great-grandmother among them, and then he killed them, and built the first shrine to Woden in her place before they made the one on the harbor island. Our grandmother told us that story when I was ten years old, how she had to watch them kill her mother while she was just a child. Cynethryth and I swore we would tell the story to our granddaughters to let them know that the goddess of the forest has taken her revenge on the line of Frisian kings by killing the children of the tribe. But Cynethryth did not keep her oath, and I have no granddaughter, Lady, and then you came, and the men think that Woden and Frey smile on us now, but I know you work Gefean's magic, and appease her wrath."

Hildeburh sat close to the older woman, feeling the outline of her wizened body through the thin cloak she wore. She slid her arm through Modthryth's, and said in a low voice, "The vengeance of the goddess can be terrible. Odin hates women, Modthryth, because they make life, and he can only make death, like the men who worship him."

I sound like Bruna, she thought to herself ruefully. She thought of Hoc's battle-lust, fed by the blood of the drugged and raped slave, and shivered.

A slave stood before her. "The king bids you join him, my Lady."

Hildeburh frowned and rose, pressing Modthryth's hand. "We will talk some more later."

She returned to her husband, who took her arm. "Edgtheow has news of your kin," he said quietly, and she knew by the tone of his voice that the news was bad. She looked at the Jute.

"One-Eye passed to Valhalla in the spring, noble Queen. Young Hnaef Half-Hand rules the Danes now, and he took some losses this past summer season. You know as I do that there is no love lost between Jutes and Danes, but I am sorry for your grief."

"How did the noble Hoc die?" Hildeburh asked, carefully keeping her voice steady. She was shaking with anger at Edgtheow's referring to her father as One-Eye, showing disrespect for the dead as well as for the kin of his host.

"I don't know the details, my Lady. It was a sickness of some sort, a spring fever, and the Danish witch-woman could do nothing to help him."

"Who gave you these tidings?" she asked sharply.

"A Hathobard slave that we captured last summer. He left Scyldingland during the confusion of the king's death and made his way alone across the straits, heading for his homeland, when we found him in our territory. Needless to say, he serves his former master in Valhalla now." Finn nodded approvingly.

"And my brother led the war band this summer?" Hildeburh shut grief for her father from her mind, so anxious was she to hear news, even bad news, of her home.

"Yes, Half-Hand led the Danes against the Wylfings, voyaging east for plunder and the quest to make a name for himself. The Wylfings sunk one of the Danish fleet, and Hnaef returned to Denmark with no treasure to show for his war-work."

"Hnaef is young and has many summers ahead of him," Hildeburh said more lightly than she felt. "Has he chosen a queen? And what of Hoc's wife, my mother Freawaru? I am eager for news of my girlhood home."

"I cannot help you there, Lady. But I hope our new alliance will serve to make peace between Jutes and Danes as well as between Jutes and Frisians."

"I hope that as well, Edgtheow, and you are the more welcome for saying so. If you will excuse me, husband, I would like to retire and think on my father." At Finn's nod, she left the dais and the hall.

As her eyes adjusted to the dark of the frithstowe, she made her way slowly to the queen's cambrai. He has been as good as dead to me these three years, she thought, and yet his death leaves an emptiness in my spirit. One-Eye! As if that uncivilized Jute could do as much with two as Hoc did with one.

She entered her domain quietly. Raefn was asleep on his small pallet by the fire; Wealh's gentle snores echoed from the back room. A low fire burned in the grate, and her bed was turned down.

She removed her circlet and stored it carefully in its pouch in the largest of her dowry chests. Stripping to her smock, she laid her feast clothes neatly beside the circlet and closed the lid. Then she toppled into bed and turned on her side to face the fire as she began to cry silently, thinking about Hoc and her girlhood and not knowing if she cried for her father or herself.

Was Freawaru grieving too? Her thoughts turned to her mother, so bitter and silent against her husband that last summer they had been together. What had their marriage been like, these past three years with Hildeburh gone and the curse of Freyja looming over the tribe?

Hildeburh caught herself staring at the embers of the firelight and shook herself. *No trances*, she said to herself firmly. *Not now. There is no reason. Freyja cares not for Hoc's death, which happened almost half a year ago; she rejoices in Elena's birth*. Hildeburh rose and drank some water from the jar at her bedside.

She went to her herb chest to make herself a sleeping potion and set about putting the kettle on to boil and building up the fire, moving silently through the dark cambrai so as not to disturb her sleeping child. As she waited for the water to boil, she watched Raefn sleep in the deep innocence of young childhood and found herself crying again, for the love of her son rather than the loss of her father.

He is all the world to me, she thought to herself. *I could easily die protecting him, with no regrets as long as I knew he was safe. I am never happier than when we are together and he is singing to me or babbling about our hikes through the forests and the discoveries we make*. She thought back to a day last summer when they had roamed through the woods looking for barks and wild herbs she needed for her healer's work, and they had come to a stream much like the one in the wooded hills of Scyldingland. She glowed remembering Raefn's delight when she overturned large, flat stones in the slow-moving parts of the stream to expose crayfish and salamanders.

"Just watch, Raef, don't touch. They are delicate. We have no reason to hurt them, and they are beautiful just where they are." Hildeburh felt as if she were melting into some sort of mystical maternal joy, with the sun on her back by the rippling stream in the cool summer forest, watching her son as he squatted intently at the side of the stream. In a way, she thought, this is worship of the goddess as well.

"Eat bugs." He looked up at her and made a face.

"Yes, my little prince, they do eat bugs. For many animals eat many different things, and just think how many more bugs there would be in this world to bite you if the crayfish did not eat them."

Further upstream she had shown him how to make a rough net from the long grasses that grew along the banks, and she sang him songs in Danish of the history of the Scyldings while they waited for a fish to enter their trap. She flipped the fish from the stream onto the bank right next to Raefn, and they both screamed and laughed as the fish flopped around until Raefn caught it and wrapped it in some rough cloth and stuck it in his pocket. Later that evening he had told Finn over and over, as they ate it, how he and Mama had caught the fish and brought it home for their evening meal.

Hildeburh poured her tea and rearranged Raefn's covers while it steeped. She could hear the faint sound of carousing from the hall; Finn and Edgtheow and the warriors would be drinking till sunrise.

I have a good husband, she thought to herself, *and he is dear to me if not close. He is Raefn's father, and I love him more for that than anything. My marriage is all my father could have hoped. And now he is dead, and I find myself allied to Jutes, living in a tribe where the goddess was silenced and her priestesses killed long ago. Freawaru expected worse. I expected nothing. But Freyja is kind; her acolyte is a mother, and yet her wrath is stilled, and she smiles on the Frisians and their adopted queen.*

She sat by the fire, sipping her tea, watching her son sleep, in a rare moment of quiet and solitude. Does Finn know about Gefean? He had never countenanced mention of Freyja, even as Hildeburh helped birth the babies and only one mother had died in the past two years. The one time he had struck her was on midwinter day, last winter. The men had been drinking in the hall, warming up to go to the shrine of Woden in the forest for the midwinter rites. The shrine on the harbor island was locked in ice and inaccessible. She had assumed Finn would go right to the forest—as in Scyldingland, the king and the bard were Woden's priests—but he had returned to her cambrai to pick up a cloak, or some boots, and had found her tranced in the garden, celebrating Freyja's sleep with the sacred prayers Bruna had taught her when she was fourteen.

She had sat on the cold ground in nothing but her smock, warm in Freyja's sleepy winter embrace. Her unseeing eyes actually looked on the plenty of Freyja's harvest, piled high in the garden as the birds raced round the stalks of wheat and the almost full-grown fawns walked sure-footedly next to their mothers, already growing with what would be next year's births. She was blessed to see the white elk sleeping in the cool of a winter sunlit hollow among the trees. She had not seen Adon or his lovers since the day she had spoken with Hild.

Abruptly, Freyja's world shattered, and she found herself lying on the ground of her garden, shivering and clutching at her right temple. Finn had struck her, hard, with the back of his hand, and he stood over her. She smelled mead in his beard and knew he was drunk.

"Well does Cyneheard call you a witch," he sneered at her. "Women must obey their husbands! And on Woden's day, of all days, you defy me and practice your goddess witch work in your witch garden." He strode around the garden, kicking at the stakes and supports, tramping on the beds of Freyja's herbs, and tearing vines from their trellises. She watched in silence, knowing she could repair whatever damage he might inflict, wishing he would go away, hating him in his rage.

"Frey is god of birth; Woden is All-Father to me and to this tribe. My people. And you are My Wife. Is that clear?" He clutched the front of her smock and lifted her, choking, so that their eyes were level. "There are no goddesses in Frisia, though there might be in Denmark." He let her drop, and she began crawling backwards away from him. He went inside, found whatever it was he was looking for, and left for the forest. She had not said one word the entire time.

That afternoon, she had started treating herself with Odin's bane, drinking the tea every day for almost a year. Finn expressed surprise that she hadn't become pregnant again. She did not know if he remembered that afternoon.

They probably sacrifice slaves to Woden here as well, she thought. Suddenly grief overcame her, and she put her head on her knees and wept. How could the father she had loved, and the man she had wanted to love, have done that? How could they betray her like that? Why did she remember Hoc most clearly painted with runes and raping a slave girl on the altar of Odin rather than as a gentle father who had let her play with his beard and repair his boat? Why was it that when she and Finn had haemod together all she could think about was his visits to the slave quarters, both back home and here in Frisia, and the rites of Woden that the men celebrated here?

He is a good husband, she told herself grimly. All of the men do all of those things, and perhaps he does not think of Woden's rites when we are alone together, and of course he never speaks of them. Then she looked at Raefn, and felt her heart breaking because she knew that in five years he would have his monwart, and go to the rites of Woden, and be lost to her forever in his innocence and love.

Her tears and the fire mingled in her eyes, and she felt the world receding and cried to the goddess in despair. Though she made no sound to disturb her son, she heard herself imploring, "Freyja, take me; keep me in your garden, and let me be safe with you," and the world of her vision spun; the fire becoming the depths of the forest, a place she had never been before, and she was cold.

Seven hunters came, and in the shifting light of the goddess' world they looked all to have Hoc's face, and then the light changed, and they all looked like Finn. They wore leather corslets studded with iron and carried spears and knives, and their beards and hair were matted and dirty with grease and mud and sticks. They rode ponies with long manes, carefully staying together as much as possible in the thick trees. The forest looked twilit although she somehow knew it was daytime.

The leader stopped and gestured with his spear. The white elk was roaming through the trees some distance away from them, her coat gleaming in the gloom. Although she gave no sign, Hildeburh sensed that the elk knew the hunters were there. The leader, who looked somewhat like Cyneheard when he turned his head, directed the others with hand signals until the elk was surrounded.

"Ka-yi!" he cried, and his spear flew toward the elk, who looked at him with no expression in her eyes. She felt no fear. Hildeburh screamed, though she knew even as she screamed that the elk and the hunters could not hear her. When the spear entered the elk's flank, she snorted with pain, and the blood ran in rivulets down her side.

Other spears soared towards her until all seven stuck from her body in a hideous display of blood. She rolled her eyes, snorted again, and sank to her knees as the blood ran out of the wounds, watering the earth beneath. As her body collapsed on a bed of dried leaves, she closed her eyes and lay still.

The men came toward her cautiously, unsheathing their knives. There was no glint of steel; the iron knives were dull and lacklustre. Each man put his hand on the shaft of his spear and prepared to draw it from the body. As his fingers closed around the smooth, dark wood, he froze immobile.

Sunlight split the trees as the wind picked up force. Leaves gusted up from the earth, whirling through the tableau of the frozen hunters and the dead elk. Then the light changed, and the figures of the hunters and their spears grew lambent, then translucent, and finally the wind blew them away as it blows pine needles from the surface of a pond.

Hildeburh watched the elk sleeping on the leaves in the forest. No wounds marred the smooth beauty of her body. The elk's eyes opened, and she rose and came towards Hildeburh.

Hildeburh held out her hands in supplication, recalling her prayer to be taken to the garden forever. The elk stood in front of her and placed her soft nose in Hildeburh's hands.

Currents of delight and power and awe rippled up through her arms as the elk nuzzled Hildeburh's hands, her warm moist breath gentling and assuaging her grief. Then she began licking her hands, and Hildeburh stood absolutely still in wonder as the elk licked each palm and finger with a smooth tongue, making an odd humming noise at the same time. Then, with another snort, she melted back into the forest.

The sunlight shining through the trees gradually reasserted itself as firelight, and Hildeburh realized with disappointment that she was back in her cambrai, not still in the garden. Her body was stiff and cold from sitting so long curled up with her head on her knees; she had trouble moving at first and gingerly raised her head and straightened out her arms. As she extended her hands towards the fire, she saw that her palms and fingers where the elk had licked them were bright blue.

Chapter Seven

M odthryth's body lay crumpled in the dirt of the turnip bed, the digging stick still clutched in her stiffened hand. Elena hid behind Hildeburh. She had seen the old woman fall earlier in the morning and had run to get the queen.

Wealh and Hildeburh hoisted the corpse between them and carried it into Modthryth's cambrai. The interior was dark and dirty. The dirt floor had not been swept and the women's boots, wet with late summer rain, formed small puddles of mud on the floor. They placed her body on the bed, musty old straw covered with sour and stained weavings. Modthryth's loom was caked with dust and mildew; she hadn't been able to see well enough to weave for a number of years. Hildeburh opened one of the two storage chests; it contained some basic garden tools and an undyed smock. The other chest was empty.

"A grim end, my Lady," said Wealh.

"I imagine she gave most of her things to her son's wives after Offa died. But this is dreary beyond belief." Hildeburh looked into the hearth. Dead coals filled the back of the fireplace; Modthryth had not had a fire to warm her on her last night on earth, and probably many previous as well.

"Get the blue cloak from my middle chest," Hildeburh said as she gazed at the grey and wrinkled face of the woman who had held the jar of Freyja's tea for her when Raefn was born. "Bring my small herb chest and the mending kit. And don't say a word to anyone about this. Modthryth is not yet ready to meet the tribe in death." Wealh nodded and left.

Finn had left Ceolfrith and Cuthbert in charge of the hall earlier that summer as the eagle-prowed ships made ready to leave the harbor. By now, the Frisian fleet would have met with Edgtheow and his Jutes at the mouth of the Eider river and attacked the Eiders and then the Hathobards. Hnaef had sent word that he would not interfere; the Danes were heading for Britain.

Ceolfrith and Cuthbert did little but sit in the hall all day, drinking mead and issuing orders to the women and children. Supposedly they were Frey's priests that summer, chosen to oversee the fertility of the land and the women, but Hildeburh had found in her summers in Frisia that Frey's anointed were often little more than a nuisance

as they questioned and argued her decisions about the
frithstowe, the livestock, and the tribal fields. She had
ignored Cuthbert's order to plant only wheat instead of
a mixture of wheat and oats; the ponies had to eat next
winter, and Ceolfrith and Cuthbert wouldn't know the
difference even if they bothered to check the plants in the
fields.

If they knew that Modthryth had died, they would
summarily order her body burnt and her ashes buried
without ceremony, for they feared the evil spirits associated
with the dead body of a woman, any woman, but especially
an old and widowed one.

"Why does this cambrai smell so bad, Queen?"
Hildeburh had forgotten Elena, sitting quietly on the
floor.

"Modthryth died with no kin, Elena, and there was no
one to care for her. What would Aescher do if the slaves
did not clean Ludhild's cambrai?"

"He would be very angry," Elena said solemnly.

"And don't you or one of your brothers or sisters go to
Ludhild's every morning to bring her fresh water and new
wood, and light her fire, and tell her you love and honor
her?"

"Oh, yes."

"Well, Modthryth's husband and sons all died in
summer raids, so there was no one to be angry at the slaves
for not doing their work here. Her two daughters-in-law

died giving birth before I came here, and her youngest son never married, so she had no grandchildren to bring her the things she needed and for her to love and tell stories to.

"I feel I have failed her, Elena, for I should have realized long ago that she was without kin, and as queen I should have made sure she was taken care of. The least I can do now is to give her a good death. No one else will."

"Why did she die?"

Hildeburh looked at Modthryth's body. "I think her heart stopped working because she was old and hadn't been eating enough food and she was probably cold and weak. Look at this." She crossed to the fireplace. Modthryth's kettle hung from its iron chain. The inside was dry and grimy. It had not been used for some time.

"Take this to the well, and wash it out thoroughly. Fill it and bring it back. We'll need to wash her body before she goes to the spirit world." As she handed the kettle to Elena, Hildeburh saw her own blue palm, faded to a light blue now, and was reminded of the night five years before when Modthryth had told her what little she knew of Gefean the forest goddess. It was strange that days or even weeks could go by without her noticing or thinking about her blue hands and what they meant, especially considering the furor they had initially caused.

It had been the first time Hildeburh had consciously lied to her husband. She had told him that dyeing the skin was a Scylding rite of mourning for a king. Since Finn had no way to disprove what she said, he had accepted the explanation despite his suspicions but seemed unnerved whenever he saw her, especially when he had to take something from her hands. But as the color had faded, life had resumed its normal rhythms, and Hildeburh realized that the story Modthryth had told her was so old none of the other Frisians knew it. No one even vaguely associated blue hands with an ancient woman's power that had been crushed by the All-Father and his minions. Cyneheard still railed against her occasionally, but Hildeburh didn't think even he knew the story of the destruction of the forest shrine and the slaughter of the priestesses.

And now Modthryth was dead, and no one knew the story but Hildeburh. She began removing Modthryth's smock, peeling off the stiff and dirty wool.

After Wealh and Elena returned, Hildeburh washed the body with boiled lavender water and sewed the blue cloak into a shroud. "Tell two of the field slaves to dig a grave in the north hill and build a pyre. Elena, now you can tell the thanes' wives that Modthryth is dead. Start with your mother. We will see her off tonight with all ceremony." *It will be good for all of us to have some sort of celebration, anyway*, she thought. She had just posted daily lookouts on the headlands to watch for the men's return, and an air of anxious expectation of the landing was beginning to set in.

That evening she stood at the foot of the pyre. It was a mat of woven reeds suspended over a grave filled with kindling and logs. Modthryth lay on her side, her body curled as it had been when she lay in her mother's womb many years before. Her mother earth would receive her in the same position. The late evening sun shot its rays through the forest as the shadows deepened over the group of women and children around the pyre.

Hildeburh wore a simple gold circlet and held the torch. "Modthryth, widow of Offa, mother of Eomer, Sigurd, and Thorkel, lady of Frisia, we salute your passing. With you we bury your loom weights and shuttles." Hildeburh nodded to Elena, who placed them on the pyre. "And your gardening tools. But we do not bury your memory. Wife of a good thane, mother to three more good thanes, keeper of your cambrai, maker of cloth, and teller of stories, we remember you."

The little ones were restless, wanting to go inside for the feast of fish and fresh berries they had been promised. Many of the women were whispering among themselves, not listening to the queen's words. Hildeburh realized, with a wrench, that no one cared. Even Ceolfrith and Cuthbert, who had been out hunting all day, had expressed little interest in the funeral and had not bothered to attend. She was the only person to whom Modthryth's death mattered at all. She touched the torch to the reeds of the pyre and then thrust it into the grave to ignite the logs beneath. As orange, yellow, and red flames consumed the pyre and climbed into the darkness, Hildeburh quietly sang the death song to Modthryth, thinking that Modthryth would appreciate it the most of all the Frisians.

> *Take her, goddess, to the garden*
> *Take her where the flowers grow*
> *Take her where the sun will shine*
> *Take her where Freyja's peace will go*

There was a crash as the reed mat gave way and the shroud fell into the grave. The flames roared, and the women started leading their children down the hill to the hall. Hildeburh was left alone with the two slaves who would tend the fire until it burnt itself out.

No one cares that she is gone, she thought to herself again. The hair on her arms stood up and tingled with apprehension as she realized that her funeral could very well be the same or worse. She was still a stranger in the land. Viking life meant that she would likely outlive her husband, since she had proved she probably would not die in childbirth. When Finn died, she would be mother to the king, if Raefn had grown to manhood. Hildeburh imagined, briefly, the way she would feel to hear the news that Raefn had been killed in battle, far from home, his body drowned in a watery grave or left on a battlefield for the animals to pick at. A wail escaped from her mouth as she suddenly felt that loss, infinitely greater than the loss of her husband, and she fell on her knees before the roaring flames and cried, for she had known, however briefly and fleetingly, a mother's grief for a dead child and wondered that Modthryth had lived through the deaths of all three of her children.

The goddess takes as well as gives, she reminded herself. Bruna tried to teach me that, but it is hard, and I have forgotten much of what she taught me. Hildeburh had not kept up most of the seasonal rituals for Freyja since Finn had found her in a trance and torn up her garden; she clearly remembered only the chants for the medicines she used regularly, and tranced only to boil her hands before a birth. She had not had visions since the night she had learned of her father's death.

The slaves began pushing the earth back into the grave, extinguishing the coals and covering the charred cloth and tools. Maybe it is time to have another child, she thought. A new life to cherish and teach and hold. The goddess takes but also gives. And then maybe there will be someone who sorrows when I go to Freyja's garden for good. She thought of the sour-tasting tansy tea of Odin's Bane and felt relief that she wouldn't drink it anymore. She was sure she would become pregnant soon after the men returned; it hadn't taken long last time.

The men's return meant another loss for her as well, one she had tried not to think about that summer. Raefn had turned seven, and he would become a man on the magic day of autumn when the night and the day were the same length. They had only a moon and a half left together, and then he would no longer sleep in her cambrai on his little bed next to the fire. Worry about that when it happens, she said to herself.

She rose and wiped her face with her hands, straightened her circlet on her forehead, and headed down the hill to the hall, where Modthryth's funeral feast was already well underway. Cuthbert and Ceolfrith had obviously quickly disposed with the formalities concerning Modthryth and Frey and proceeded directly to the mead and food. Some of the slaves were supervising children's games at the far end of the hall. Hildeburh pulled her shoulders back and entered the hall to take her place next to Finn's empty gift-throne.

Almost a moon-cycle later, Finn was back, his gift-throne no longer empty, and his loud voice rang through the hall as the warriors recounted the summer's viking raids for the benefit of Cuthbert and Ceolfrith. Finn had presented each of them with Hathobard slave girls, silver torques, and new swords to be used the following summer when they would no longer be priests of Frey but Finn's warriors once again. Their honor satisfied, Ceolfrith and Cuthbert listened as Cyneheard sang of the voyage down the Eider river and the skirmishes and raids along the way. The Eider valley had yielded to Finn with little resistance; the sight of the eagle ships drove most of the peoples into hiding while the Frisians took what they wanted from the abandoned settlements.

Hildeburh had passed the cup to Finn's captains and then stood watching her husband at the side of his throne. Even by torchlight she could see that the lines around his eyes had deepened, and the hair on his temples was growing in grey. His skin was deeply tanned by the summer sun. He still wore only black tunics, very short, to show off his firm and muscled legs. Finn's stomach was flat again from the summer on the sea and the river; like the other men, he would put on some weight over the winter.

She had been formal with him since the return late that morning, when she had stood on the harbor beach with Raefn in the front of the crowd of women and children. Ceolfrith and Cuthbert greeted Finn and transferred his kingly power back to him. He had nodded to her and greeted her plainly before grasping Raefn's forearms and giving him a formal warrior's greeting, king to prince.

"I have returned, my son, and rejoice to see that you are well."

Hildeburh had primed Raefn for this moment, his father's first experience of him as a young man rather than a child. For Hildeburh, Raefn would always be a child, who hunted for salamanders and climbed trees and rode the ponies barebacked over the headlands and beaches. For Finn, Raefn was the prince, the young man he would train to be king someday. Yet her heart swelled with pride and relief when Raefn looked into his father's face and said, clear and loud, "All Frisia rejoices at your successful return, my Father and King. Welcome home."

"I have brought many things back to Frisia, treasure for each of my warriors, goods and cloth for your mother, and even a sword, something on the smallish side, for you. You will receive it in the hall tonight, and you must train with it all winter, for next summer you will come with me, and we will journey together, father and son, king and prince, as I did with Folcwalda, my father, king before me."

Finn had brought the sword to the feast and was now giving it to Raefn. Odin's raven was inlaid in obsidian on the hilt. "To the prince named for the raven of wisdom that counsels Odin, I give this sword taken this summer. May you use it well for our people." Aescher and Handschue led the cheering as Raefn stepped on the dais next to his father to accept the sword. They have prospered with Finn as well, thought Hildeburh as she watched Finn's two closest thanes.

Finn began distributing treasure to his men, the primary activity of the homecoming feast. All of the takings were technically the king's, and he then distributed them as he saw fit, to reward and strengthen loyalty or to give indication of his pleasure or displeasure with a warrior's service. Aescher and Handschue received the largest and most precious gifts first. Hildeburh watched and waited; the gift giving and toasting would go on until day started to break in the eastern sky. The litany of swords, arm-rings, pony saddles and torques, mingled with brief references to raids and landings and rowing prowess, began to swim before her eyes.

She must have fallen asleep on her low chair at the side of the dais, for Wealh was shaking her, and Finn was bidding his men goodnight. She rose and left the hall with her husband. In the predawn darkness he slipped his arm around her waist and whispered, "And finally a special greeting for you, my princess," and she suddenly felt close to him in a way she hadn't since Raefn was three summers old.

"I'm glad you're back, husband," was all that she said, but she pressed her body against his as they made their way to her cambrai.

She had directed Wealh to sleep in the hall with Raefn, so she and Finn were alone when they entered. While her loom still dominated one wall, spectacular weavings adorned the others. In the bright long summer nights of Frisia, Hildeburh had found yet another way she was Freawaru's daughter, and her weavings were sumptuous with gold cord and thick and thin wools in rich blues and greens. Her favorite dye came from tiny, bright blue mushrooms that grew only in the spring, and she used the blue wool for patterns of texture and shape to border her tapestries.

For the tapestry above her bed she had embroidered the goddess Neursa, wearing pearls in her hair and strung around her neck as she lay in the surf, the marine blue of the ocean waves swirling to cover all her body except her shoulders and head.

Finn threw himself on the featherbed below the tapestry of Neursa and sighed with exhaustion and delight. "Oh, Hildeburh. I thought you were insane when you started saving duck feathers, but there isn't a man in Frisia more comfortable than I am right now. You can't know how good this feels after a summer spent sleeping on a boat bench."

"Was it a rough summer, Finn?" she asked as she perched next to him in her smock.

"No. It was boring, actually. We show up, and they run away. Edgtheow and his Jutes were good allies—they protected our backs once when we met a fleet of Geats in the straits, and their ships made our fleet look that much stronger. We didn't even have to do that much fighting. I now control all of the lands of the North Sea, Hildeburh. They all answer to me." He folded his arms behind his head and looked up at her.

"You are as darkly beautiful as ever, my princess. Welcome me home." He reached under her smock and pulled her towards him with both hands. She could still smell sea salt and mead in his beard when he kissed her and his beard caressed her cheek as his hands rubbed her breasts and her thighs. Quickly, he pulled off his tunic and mounted her, the smock pushed up around her waist to reveal her belly white and flat in the firelight. He entered her quickly and slid his arms around her back, crushing her to him, and she smelled again the salt in his chest hair and felt the odd smoothness of the hairless part of his shoulder and remembered—yes, this is what it is like. She felt an odd detachment about haemod, almost as if she were watching herself and Finn perform a ritual instead of participating in it. Now I move my hips. Now he moves his faster. Now he groans twice—no, three times, it was a good one—and now he buries his face in my neck.

He rolled over and rubbed his groin with one of the bed weavings before settling back in the bed and closing his eyes. "Hildeburh," he said groggily, "it's good to be home." She watched the firelight dance as her husband began to snore.

The days flew after the men's return as the Frisians gathered in the final harvest, slaughtered cattle, repaired the boats, and laid in stocks of firewood for the long winter ahead. There had been no deaths or serious wounds from the summer journey; Hildeburh's healing skills were not needed, and the final baby of the season was born easily a week after the return. She tried to do as much as possible with Raefn, beginning in her mind to count the days they had left together. And Raefn slept in the hall almost every night as she and Finn came together as husband and wife, trying, as he said, "for another prince to lead Frisia."

All too soon came the day of Raefn's monwart, and Lyda and Hildeburh stood with the other mothers of seven year old boys. They watched Brecc and Raefn as they ran in the open area before the hall, playing at being vikings and acting out the stories they heard Cyneheard sing in the hall. Suddenly, Brecc swatted Raefn and knocked him down.

Outraged, Raefn glared at his friend. "You can't hit me! I'm going to be your king!" He leapt up and flung himself at Brecc, and the two of them rolled on the ground, struggling.

"Brecc, Raefn!" Hildeburh said sharply. "You may not fight among yourselves. This is not seemly behavior for a prince. Stand up, and wait for the king's approach."

The boys stopped, and Raefn looked at his mother. "You can't tell me what to do anymore, mother. Father says that I am a man now, and I don't have to listen to any woman."

Hildeburh was stunned into silence. Her little boy, still with baby fat on his cheeks, had defied her in front of the tribe. And she could do nothing. Her hands clenched, and she said grimly, "Respect for the woman who raised you is kingly behavior, Raefn, and I'm sure your father would agree." *Though I'm not sure,* she admitted to herself. She knew that for Finn, she existed on the outskirts of life, a vague presence of comfort with her featherbed, necessary for bearing another heir and passing the cup in the hall. Haemod he could get anywhere—and he did—she had no illusions that he considered her special and was not interested in other women. For Finn, the focus of life was fighting, hunting, and drinking with his men.

Today, Raefn would become one of those men, and she would move from the center to the outskirts of his life as well. She felt her throat closing up as she fought back more tears, for she had wept silently most of the night for the son who was to become a stranger to her. She needed to look calm now before the tribe.

Slaves flung open the main doors of the hall, and Finn strode through them. He looked like Thor as the old songs described him, with his black tunic, red-brown beard, and jeweled sword and hammer. Finn wore his richest circlet and an enormous torque. His arms were covered with arm rings and there were even ankle bracelets above his bare feet. He was followed by Aescher, Brecc's father, and the other fathers of seven year old boys; the rest of the men lagged behind in a larger group, many still clutching their ivory mead horns. Hildeburh didn't see Cyneheard, but she assumed he was there at this most important occasion of a prince's monwart on the magic day of autumn.

"Where is my son, the prince, Raefn of Frisia?" Finn's voice boomed across the compound although he could see Raefn perfectly well right in front of him. Hildeburh had seen the beginning of the monwart ritual six times now and knew what was coming. She bit her tongue and thought about how much it hurt so she wouldn't cry. After this ceremony, she would no longer be Raefn's mother in the eyes of the tribe.

"Here I am, Father and King," Raefn answered dutifully.

"Are you ready to don the tunic and breech of manhood and set aside the smock of childhood? Are you ready to bear arms for your king and the glory of your people? Are you ready to pledge blood to your father?"

"Yes, father, I am ready," he answered.

Finn crossed the open space to his son and removed his sword from its scabbard. He separated the rings on his left forearm and slit the tender inside skin revealed there so that blood welled to the surface. Then he took Raefn's right arm and made an identical cut. Hildeburh watched, wanting to shriek out—don't hurt him—and then wanting to gather her son to her and kiss his hair and tell him he would be fine; he was brave—when Raefn winced and blinked back tears as the cut began to sting and burn and bleed. Finn gripped his son's elbows so that their forearms touched and their blood mingled.

"We are of one blood, now, Raefn. Your blood is mine. I am a man, and you are now as well. Come with me to Woden's shrine and learn the mysteries of manhood from your father as befits a future king."

Raefn was excited, the pain forgotten. He knew that this monwart meant his first ride in his father's eagle boat to the small island in the harbor where Odin's shrine was protected by water on all sides. He did not look back at his mother as Finn and he started down the path to the harbor and the other fathers began their ritual questioning and cutting of their sons.

Hildeburh walked slowly back to her cambrai. She entered and sat on her bed and stared at the floor. The quiet engulfed her. He was gone.

Wealh came in, took one look at Hildeburh, and started chattering and bustling about to dispel the gloom. She made up the fire, put on the kettle, made the bed, and shook out the tapestries in the garden. She stocked the log box and rearranged the contents of one of the dowry chests, talking all the while. "In my country, my Lady, we had a similar ceremony. I don't remember the name of it anymore, since I know my mother tongue no longer. Isn't that odd? I wonder if I will be able to talk to my ancestors in the afterlife or if I will just speak Frisian gibberish to them. But I remember our chief, wearing a great bearskin cloak and carrying a rod of power, and he touched each boy with the rod, and its magic changed him from a boy to a man. Then the new men would go, with some of the older men, and hunt for boar, and some days later they would come back, exhausted and hungry because they couldn't eat or drink anything until they had hunted successfully. They would come back to the village, all carrying the boar trussed on big stakes, singing. We would feast them that night as men—and they ate like men, after fasting for two or three days.

"Mistress," Wealh said gently, "he is gone, but he is happy and healthy. His father loves him, in Finn's own way. He has not been killed in a battle or eaten by a wolf or maimed in a fall. You will see him and talk to him in the hall. He is not wholly lost to you. I miss him too, but it is time for life to change. Maybe it is time for you to have another baby."

"You're right, Wealh. It's not like he's dead." I am grieving for his growing up and growing away, but also for my own life in a society where I am both strange and useless. I do not matter. Any female body would suffice as queen here. Hnaef isn't strong enough to threaten Finn at all, so even the political reason for my marriage has become insignificant. Hnaef is actually just another of Finn's client kings, like Edgtheow, and I am not needed to keep the peace.

"And we do need another baby. I'll call you, Wealh, if I need anything. I just want to be alone right now." Wealh nodded and left.

Hildeburh stared into space, numb in her loss. The past seven years of her life had been devoted almost wholly to her son, and now he was gone from her. She didn't want to think about the rites on Odin's island, about her child watching or even participating in something like the spring ritual she had watched over ten summers before in Denmark. What were they killing for him to grow hard and brutal upon? She didn't want to know.

"Goddess." She spoke aloud, to Freyja or Gefean she didn't know which, for the two melded in her dreams sometimes. "Don't let me lose him utterly. Let part of me remain with him." For the first time since she had learned of her father's death, she tried to go into a visionary trance; unlike the brief, almost brusque trance she could induce almost immediately to purify her hands before attending a birth, a visionary trance came slowly and made her feel slightly dizzy at the beginning. She wanted to see herself and Raefn in the future. The room was spinning, the firelight was glowing. Hildeburh whispered to herself, "taste the flowers and the fruit, see the flowers and the fruit..."

For a brief moment, she saw the three dancing girls, then darkness fell again as she heard their voices, echoing laughter and crying Adon's name in exultation, then she saw the white elk trotting through a meadow, then a bonfire at night ringed by women wearing blue smocks. She longed to join them, and briefly glimpsed their tattooed faces and heard their wondrous chant before she felt herself falling from a cliff into the sea, and she screamed just before she hit the waves and the rocks beneath—they were covered with skulls, and she knew they were skulls of women.

Hildeburh found herself on her hearth in her cambrai, shaking and drenched in sweat. Wealh ran into the room. "Mistress, are you sick?" She lifted Hildeburh and helped her to the bed.

"Sick in my spirit, I think. I'll be fine." Hildeburh managed a slight smile. I cannot go there, she thought. It has been so long I have forgotten the way. Her mind numbed with the double loss of Raefn and the goddess, she fell into a fitful sleep of boredom.

When she awoke it was twilight, the sky a deep blue with the first stars shining in the firmament. The faint sound of singing wafted through the night air from the hall; the men, including Raefn, were feasting tonight without women or children. She rose and went into the garden, the packed earth cool on her bare feet, the shadows on the plants sharp in the bright light of the just-risen moon. She plucked one of the last blades of autumn wheat from its stalk and laid it reverently on the earth.

"Freyja, Gefean, by all your names I implore you, Mother Goddess of earth and air and water and fire, forgive me, your priestess, for neglecting your worship. Forgive me for fearing the wrath of my husband more than the pain of your neglect; forgive me for accepting the rules and ways of men so that knowledge of your power wanes like the shrinking moon.

"By this waxing moonlight, goddess, I swear to be true to you for the rest of my life. My son is lost to me, and I no longer need to protect myself to protect him. I am yours, Freyja, and if a child now grows in my womb, that child will be yours as well, whether boy or girl."

She took her knife from her pocket and unsheathed it. Its blade gleamed in the moonlight as she re-cut the old scars of her initiation fifteen summers before. She made sure the cuts were deep, for the pain was a prelude to the pain of childbirth, the blood spilled to water the land as blood of the mother spilled when the baby came from her body. She squeezed the cuts to make dark patches on the earth of her garden.

Then she sat quietly, cross legged, and gazed at the moon and smelled the last of the late summer flowers and the tang of the sea in the night air. The wind blew off the waves she could hear but not see, and it seemed to her exhausted and wrung out heart and ears that the wind whispered, "yes," as it blew from the sea to the inland forest of pines.

Chapter Eight

Hildeburh stood before Finn's hall, issuing orders to the kitchen slaves. Edgtheow had come in the middle of the day, rushing up the path from the beach with the sentry, demanding to see Finn. Hildeburh's heart chilled when she heard him muttering about "Half-Hand" and "Scyldings," but Finn had peremptorily ordered her from the hall to arrange a feast in honor of his client king. As Hildeburh gave instructions about fish and breads and stews, her mind raced over the possible meanings of Edgtheow's coming. Was Hnaef dead? And could she get news of her people?

She finished the feast plans, and the group of six or seven slaves fell silent as a young woman made her way from the harbor path towards them. Her skin shone pale and white even after the sun of summer, and her light brown-red hair cascaded down her back in an ocean of curls and ringlets.

Her green smock matched her green eyes. She carried a basket of clothes she had just washed in the sea.

Cynna stared at the queen and the group of slaves but did not speak to them. She shifted the basket from one hip to the other and the motion created flashes of brilliance as the sun spangled on the jeweled bracelets on both wrists. Matching bracelets banded her ankles, and a carved ivory comb held the curls off her face. She angled off to the right side of the hall, where Finn had made a special door leading to the king's chamber just for her.

Hildeburh's cheeks burned, and she suddenly felt old, tired, and ugly, as she often did when confronted by the sight of her husband's sixteen-year-old favorite. In her twenty-eighth autumn, Hildeburh knew that her taut belly, slim hips, and unlined face were not coming back. "Are there any questions?" she asked curtly. "Then that is all. Be prepared to start serving before the sun goes below the trees."

She turned and walked quickly to her cambrai, which was fast becoming her sole refuge in Friesland. It was almost time for Higd to awake from her midday rest, and Hildeburh liked to be there for her daughter's drowsy sweetness. She sat quietly, spinning wool in the semi-darkness until Higd stirred and stretched and then, seeing her mother, stumbled from her pallet into Hildeburh's lap to wake fully in her mother's embrace.

"Mama, we go fishing?" Higd loved fishing, in the streams of the forest or in the tidepools and shallows of the harbor.

"Not today, sweet. This afternoon we work in the garden, and then tonight there is a feast in the hall."

Hildeburh gave Higd a drink of water from the jar by her bed and fished a honeycake from her pocket for her. Then they went into the garden and knelt in the center of the beds, which radiated from the fire and cauldron in the middle like the rays of the sun. Some beds grew Freyja's herbs, and Higd knew not to touch them, and some grew tubers and vegetables. In one Hildeburh and Higd had planted berry plants, and Higd's delight when the berries were large and ripe enough to eat compensated for the repeated trips to the well to keep the soil damp in the bright, long, sunny days of the northern summer.

"You start," Hildeburh whispered.

"Mother Goddess Freyja, bless our work in your earth today," Higd said clearly.

"Let our spirits and bodies be as fruitful as your earth," Hildeburh finished. They rose to begin harvesting greens, carefully shaking the rich loam from the roots before placing them in a collecting basket.

Three autumns before, Hildeburh had stood on the beach watching the ships come in, her baby girl in her arms. The ceremony of acceptance and naming of the summer babies was held the day after landing; most of the warriors were still woozy from the toasts of the gift-giving feast the night before. Hildeburh had known that Finn was disappointed, from the eager way he strode towards her from the ship and the slackening of his pace and his smile when she called to him that the baby was a princess, not a prince as he had hoped. But she had felt only relief when Lyda and Wealh had exclaimed "a girl"—no loss, no monwart for this one.

Finn could order the baby exposed, though, and the worry had gnawed at her the rest of the summer as she waited for her husband to return. None of the Frisian men had refused to name a child in the seven years she lived in Friesland, but Wealh had told her of it, thanes with too many daughters for fathers who didn't want any more. At the naming ceremony Finn looked at his baby girl, while Hildeburh's heart lurched in the moment of silence, and she felt sure he would order the baby placed in the forest. Then the baby saw the pearls gleaming on her father's arm-rings, and she smiled and reached for the shininess, and Finn smiled too, and Hildeburh almost cried with relief.

"I name you Higd, my daughter, for you are very wise to reach for your father and his bright pearls." Hildeburh nodded as the women behind her began to present their babies, one by one, to their fathers for names and acceptance within the tribe.

But Finn had not returned to her cambrai that fall or since. He slept in the king's chamber by himself, often calling one of the slaves in for haemod with the king. One of them had borne a daughter last summer and claimed it was the king's, but Finn had not named the child, and she was growing up a slave with her mother. Hildeburh knew that Finn was no longer interested in her, in her body that produced only infrequently, in her ideas of birth and healing and counsel, or in her people and their place in his world. She thought sometimes that he might take another wife, or contrive to send her away; more often she told herself that her presence made life easy for him, as she quietly managed the hall and the frithstowe, greeted his guests and raised his daughter, and reassured herself repeatedly against her greatest fear, that he would send her away from her children.

She showed Higd how to unwind a bean vine from its stake and remove the stake from the bed, thinking all the while about the conference going on in the hall. How did Hnaef fit into Edgtheow's unexpected arrival?

Finally, when the sun was low enough and half of the beds had been prepared for winter, Hildeburh and Higd washed in the cistern by the fence before changing their clothes and making their way to the hall. After placing Higd in the charge of a slave at the lower end of the hall, Hildeburh proceeded towards the dais.

Finn sat on his throne, laughing. He lightly held a mead horn in one hand and with the other caressed Cynna's thighs. She stood to the side of the throne, within easy reach of her master's wandering hands. He looked at Edgtheow, not at Cynna, though, and Hildeburh saw that Cynna was just as unimportant to the real business of Finn's life as she was.

Finn saw her coming and gently shoved Cynna away; she obediently took a seat on one of the benches massed against the wall. The thanes were already assembled, and the women and children were coming in. "Hildeburh," Finn said, "please welcome our guest to the feast."

She nodded and took the large cup handed to her by a slave. "Welcome once again to Frisia, Edgtheow, where our harbor is full, our stores are ready for winter, and peace and plenty overflow in Finnsburgh, the frithstowe of Finn, king of the northern and western seas and the lands of the northern rivers. We salute your coming," she finished, and passed the cup to Finn, then Edgtheow, then Aescher and Handschue and Cyneheard and Edgtheow's Jutes.

She was about to make her way from the dais when Finn stopped her and said, "Wait. There's more." He stood, and his powerful frame seemed to fill the room with his kingly presence. There were gray streaks in his beard. Hildeburh glanced at Raefn, sitting on a bench with some of the other older boys, but he was looking at Finn, not at her.

"Edgtheow brings news of an alliance broken," Finn said carefully to the company. "Just eight days ago a group of ships beached in Jutland in the evening as darkness fell. Like thieves rather than warriors, the troop stole much of the winter stores of Edgtheow's people. They took grain and vegetables and cheese and dried meat. A slave discovered them rummaging through the storehouses and gave the alarm; they made their escape, and the Jutes could not pursue them, having already beached their boats for fall repairs. But before they escaped, Edgtheow saw them and their ships—and he saw Hnaef Half-Hand of the Scyldings sailing off in a ship with a dragon in the front."

Hildeburh had known, before he finished, who the raiders were, who came like thieves to steal food rather than like warriors to fight and win treasure and plunder. If her brother was stealing food this late in the season, it meant her people were starving and he was desperate.

"We will replace the stores you lost, Edgtheow, so that your people will not suffer this winter," Finn said, obviously announcing the agreement he and Edgtheow had worked out earlier. "Gunnar and Eric, our priests of Frey this past summer, will see the supplies sorted and packed tomorrow." The men nodded their assent as Finn glanced toward their bench. "In the spring I will send a message to Hnaef Half-Hand to tell him our alliance is broken and he must beware the wrath of Finn of Frisia and his allies." He raised his hands above his head. "The alliance with the Danes has been broken," he declared, "and the people of Half-Hand are our enemies."

Aescher leapt up and stood on his bench, his mead horn held high to echo Finn's upstretched arms. "I pledge the destruction of our enemies the Danes!" he cried, and drained his horn. The other Frisian warriors followed suit, and in a matter of moments the hall was full of shouting, drinking men, standing on the benches and proclaiming loyalty to Finn and hatred of the Danes. Hildeburh watched in horror.

Cyneheard raised himself on his crutch and looked at her with spite in his eyes. "The Dane!" he cried, his bardic voice still strong even in his old age. "The Dane! She shall leave this hall!"

Finn stood and watched, an odd gleam in his eye and half a smile on his face. Hildeburh realized in a flash that Finn had anticipated if not planned this; it was an honorable way to dispose of an inconvenience in his life, which was what she had become. Hildeburh met Cyneheard's gaze and said nothing, knowing that her husband was not going to help her. Edgtheow watched as well, and gradually the noise died away, leaving Cyneheard's words ringing in the air. In the silence, he repeated, quietly, menacingly, "The Dane shall leave this hall."

Suddenly, Raefn stood on his bench, knocking over some of the other boys in his urgency. Like his father, he wore only black, and the raven-hilted sword hung at his belt. His dark hair and tanned skin made him look dashing, and older and stronger than he really was. "The Dane," said Raefn hotly, "is my mother. And anyone who wants her to leave must deal with me first." He drew his sword and looked around the hall, studiously avoiding his father's eyes. "Anyone?"

Finn laughed and pulled Hildeburh next to him on the dais. "Spoken like a man, my prince. But this Dane is now a Frisian. She has lived among us in Finnsburgh for more than ten winters now. Her husband and children are here, and her loyalties lie with us. Hildeburh is a Frisian queen, not a Danish princess. Now, Cyneheard, how about a song? Let us celebrate our alliance and dream of springtime when we can be true warriors together again."

As the song started, Hildeburh slipped through the shadows out the door and towards her cambrai. Saved by her son, who still loved her despite his growing manhood. Hot tears blurred her vision as she entered her domain and began rummaging through her herb chest. She shook some dried mushrooms from a burlap pouch, her hands shaking as well, and as she ground them into a powder she prayed that they hadn't lost their magic in the twelve years they had lain at the bottom of that chest. She poured water into the bowl, not bothering to boil it first, and gulped down the foul smelling fungus water. I must see my brother, she thought. Please, Goddess, for the priestess who has been true to you these past four years, please let me see Hnaef and know how my people fare. I am not a Frisian queen. I am a Danish princess, no matter what my husband says.

She breathed deeply and stared into the fire. The shaking stopped, and the thunderous sound of her blood pumping in her head died down. She felt light-headed as the drug began to take effect, and she knew she would venture this time into the goddess' spirit world with the help of the magic of which Bruna had told her but which she had never used.

The firelight began to look misty. Hildeburh concentrated on Hnaef, happy times in their childhood, his face on the rock as she cut off part of his hand, their easy closeness before her marriage. The mist cleared, and Hildeburh felt she was soaring over the Danish peninsula. From above, she saw Hoc's frithstowe and the hall and the path to the beach. The boats were stored for winter against the cliffs; there were only four of them. On the harbor beach women and children in patched smocks collected seaweed in baskets. Seaweed stew, Hildeburh thought, the food of famine. I have never had to eat it. She skimmed along the surface of the air to the frithstowe, her heart sinking at the dilapidation and hardship she saw along the way yet feeling an odd elation at the movement through air. She felt like she was swimming up the path, and gave an experimental kick with her legs—yes, she did surge forward.

The burum were old. Few had been built since her departure. Some, furthest from the hall, caved in at the roof to let sunlight and rain in, and through these holes Hildeburh saw that many of the burum were empty. No mothers and children lived in them. As she passed over the edge of the compound, she saw the roof of Bruna's burum caved in and its inside full of wreckage and dirt. She gave another kick and shot towards the hall, where the deer antlers above the great doors had cracked and been re-hung in two pieces, one slightly crooked. Vines grew in the thatch roof and mud coated the gathering area before the hall.

Freawaru's burum still stood to the west side of the hall, and with longing Hildeburh steered herself toward it, yearning for her mother, hoping she could speak to her even in a vision. She peered in through a partially open shutter to see her mother, her hair now grey but still in braids, sipping tea from a wooden cup. The burum was clean but spare; many of her dowry chests were gone, the loom stood empty, and no tapestries hung on the bare walls. With a jolt, Hildeburh realized that Freawaru's companion was her old friend, Sunya. She probably wouldn't recognize me either, Hildeburh thought as she listened to Sunya, wrapped in a deerskin cloak, as she reported to the queen.

"With the Jutish supplies and the stuffs gotten in trade for the slaves, my Lady, we can all eat once a day in the hall. You and I must serve the meals to make sure that none eats more than his or her share. And Hnaef and Bjorn must assign trusted men to guard the food during the night. If we do not dole out resources carefully, my Lady, we will all die."

"We will all die anyway, Sunya." Freawaru raised her face, and Hildeburh's heart wrenched when she saw the deep lines of sorrow around her mother's eyes. "There are no children in Denmark. We are a dying race, living under Freyja's curse, and we have no priestess. Do what must be done, Sunya, but I long only to join my grandchildren in Freyja's garden. I am too old for this fight."

"Queen, please. My husband says that the White Christ greets us joyfully in death, and Bruna used to talk of Freyja's garden, and Hnaef and the bard tell us of Valhalla and Odin's feast. I don't care what awaits us after death. I want to live now. I want to have more children to take away the grief in my heart for my babies who died in last winter's hunger." Her voice cracked. "I want to live in peace and plenty again, and to do that we must get through this winter. Hnaef and Bjorn will realize that they must humble themselves before Finn and try to attach themselves to his kingship as minor allies. Then we can prosper under Finn's protection. I'd rather live under a client king than starve under a high king. So. Do I have your permission to direct the portioning of the food?"

Freawaru nodded, silent. Sunya rose and left, and Hildeburh noted the worn spots on Sunya's smock. Hnaef must not have brought home any weaving supplies from summer voyages for a long time; the few sheep the Scyldings kept for homespun wool had probably been eaten long ago. The emptiness of her mother's burum was due to famine, Hildeburh realized—Hnaef had probably traded the tapestries for food at one of the river ports. Hildeburh could only watch, much as she longed to put her arms around her mother and comfort her as Freawaru had comforted Hildeburh many years before. But flickers of firelight seeped into the edges of her vision, and she realized that her trance wavered; the magic of the mushrooms was fading. As Freawaru's image faded and wavered as well, Hildeburh clenched her teeth and prepared herself to return to her world, where there was for her no famine but still a sense of overwhelming dread.

Chapter Nine

Hildeburh spent an uneasy winter in her cambrai, teaching the rituals of Freyja to Higd and weaving tapestries. She went to the hall only once, to pass the cup at midwinter, and left soon after, unaccustomed to the noise and the smell of mead and of unwashed bodies. As she left, Finn's hands were under Cynna's dress. Lyda and the other Frisian women were laughing with their men and studiously ignoring Hildeburh. Nobody wanted to seem too friendly with the Dane, who was obviously going to be gotten rid of somehow, and soon.

Spring came before the equinox, and Hildeburh took Higd and Elene into the forest to greet Freyja on her return to Friesland. Despite Lyda's attempts to keep Elene busy and away from the queen, the little girl managed to spend part of each day with Hildeburh; Elene and Higd made baskets in Hildeburh's cambrai or dug winter tubers when the weather permitted. In all their work, Hildeburh taught the two girls to revere the goddess and her gifts. The white elk had spoken to Hildeburh on the day of Elene's birth, after all, and claimed Elene as her own.

The three of them made their way to a small clearing in the forest. Early spring sunshine spangled through the delicate green of the new-leafed trees, and the damp, cool air smelled fresh with richness and growth. Moss covered the open ground, carpeting the clearing with a spongy fuzz, and tiny white flowers hung from slender stems underneath the great pine trees.

"These trees are old, older than the stories of the blue-handed priestesses." Hildeburh had passed on Modthryth's story of Gefean to her daughter and to Elene, keeping alive the memory of the forest goddess. "They were here even before people came, and there were no rituals for her worship, when Freyja shared her magic with the animals and plants of the forest, for everything in nature is a celebration of Freyja's power."

They joined hands, Hildeburh in the center. The sun warmed her face, and the fresh air smelled clean after a winter spent indoors, full of the smoke of the fire. "I will say the words first, and then we will say them again together. Think about the gifts of growth and life as we chant, for they are Freyja's part of spring." She chanted:

Winter goes and rebirth comes
Shorter nights and warmer suns
Oats, wheat, barley, rye,
Mother's love in a newborn's eyes,
New birth comes and flowers grow,
Pine trees bud and rivers flow.
All these beauties we have seen
And thus give thanks to Freyja, Queen.

The girls joined her to chant a second time, and their high, bell-like voices rang softly in the glade. Hildeburh knew that the goddess was pleased.

Suddenly, she sensed that they were not alone, and she turned, instinctively pushing the girls behind her. She began to shake with fear when she saw Cyneheard, a notched arrow in his bow pointed straight at her heart, leaning on his crutch in front of her. His apprentice, Edgwold, stood behind him, holding a game bag.

"If Aescher's daughter were not here, I'd kill you now, you Danish devil, and please the king who has no desire other than to be rid of you. Hunters often mistake people for deer through the shadows of the trees." He lowered his bow, handed it to Edgwold, and hobbled towards her. Shepherding the whimpering girls behind her, Hildeburh backed slowly away.

"You think I don't know what you're doing here? The witch priestesses of the witch Gefean are dead—and you should be too. I know why your hands are blue, you Danish bitch, but I have not seen fit to tell my king why. Better that the very name of the witch die with me and Modthryth. I knew she knew. And my magic killed her sons before they could have daughters and she could tell them." Cyneheard's chin dripped with spittle, looking like venom as the poisonous curses started. "You will rightly die in pain like the witches before you, killed for the glory of Woden All-Father and his wolves of war. Women cannot fight. Women have no power. You are good for nothing but bearing our sons and brewing our mead." He swung his left arm across his body and struck Hildeburh across the face.

Blood erupted from her nose and mouth as her teeth cut into her lips and she fell to the ground. Cyneheard turned, saying, "My lord shall hear of this," and he made his way back towards Finnsburgh, Edgwold following him.

Hildeburh staunched the blood with the hem of her skirt, trying to soothe the terrified girls. "He will kill you, Queen," wailed Elene, and at those words Higd started to shriek. Her father had never spoken to her; she had no knowledge of him other than as a distant lord who somehow managed to make miserable the mother she adored. Hildeburh hugged and hushed them as best she could.

"We came to the forest to celebrate spring, not to be terrified by the ramblings of a nasty old man," she said as lightly as she could. "Hush. It's all right. Our goddess will protect us. Hush."

"Mama, why does Cyneheard hate you?"

"For a lot of reasons, sweetheart. I was not born here, and I brought different ideas and customs from Denmark when I came to Frisia to marry your father. And Cyneheard is a warrior, despite the loss of his leg, and warriors believe in the glory of battle and death. For if battle and death are meaningless, then the life of a warrior is meaningless too."

Hildeburh spoke slowly, trying to choose words that the five year old would understand, if only partially. Elene, at ten years old, nodded. She knew exactly what the queen meant. Hildeburh continued, "Freyja and Gefean, all-powerful goddesses of mother earth, bring life and birth and growth. Their worship has no place for war and killing. For Freyja, a loom is a much more powerful tool than a sword, and the blood of birth infinitely more precious than the blood shed in battle."

The girls quieted, and the bleeding stopped. Hildeburh knew her face was bruised, and when she got back she would take some of the ice chunks from the spring house and make a compress for her face. The way things were going, the priests of Frey for the coming summer would forbid her to attend the births of the Frisian women, and she wouldn't get to use the ice to soothe the mother after labor. Perhaps, she thought, her mind wandering, she had been using ice for so long that some of the women would ask their attendants to fetch some even if Hildeburh wasn't there.

"Let's go back," she said, carefully rising. Higd started to cry again.

"I'm scared. Let's stay here. He won't kill you here."

"We must go back, Higd. He won't kill me." Hildeburh wasn't sure if she referred to Finn or Cyneheard. "And even if he does, I will go to Freyja's garden as a spirit, and live eternally with the goddess amongst her fruit and love. I would miss you dearly, my daughter, but I would still love you, and I would be happy with the goddess. Now let's go back. We have welcomed spring, and soon the men will be gone for the summer."

As they approached the frithstowe, warriors were lighting the beacons on the corner posts of the enclosure. Slaves bustled about, and most of the men were heading towards the hall dressed in their fighting gear. Hildeburh grabbed a young boy's shoulder as he ran through the compound. "What has happened?" she demanded.

"The Danish ships have entered the harbor, queen, and the king intends to greet them as enemies, not allies." He squirmed away.

Hildeburh eagerly started toward the main gate of Finnsburgh, which opened to the gentle slope leading down to the harbor. She would see her kin! Her brother would be changed—she hadn't seen him in over twelve years. But he was her brother, and he would have all the news of home. Tonight, after the parley—for surely that was why they had come—she could sit with him in a quiet corner of the hall and hear the truth of her vision of the Danes' famine the previous autumn.

She practically ran toward the gates, anxious to see her brother, the two girls running to keep up with her. Hildeburh's heart felt light for the first time in a long time. Her brother was coming.

Her steps slowed as she reached the gates. Bjorn would be with Hnaef. *I hope he has found some sort of happiness,* she thought to herself. At the gates, Edgheard stood ready, his unsheathed sword clenched in his right hand, his boar's head helmet making him seem taller and more glorious as it shone in the glaring afternoon sun. He was Finn's third in command, after Aescher, and it was his responsibility to secure the gate to Finn's stronghold.

When he saw her, he stepped into the middle of the entrance, and faced Hildeburh as she headed towards the harbor to greet her brother.

"Finn has ordered that you not pass these gates, my Lady." His unsheathed sword glinted with sun.

"Don't be ridiculous," she snapped. "He is my brother. It would not be fitting if I were not on the beach to greet him," she said with more confidence than she felt.

"Then you must discuss that with the king, my Lady, for my orders are to keep you in Finnsburgh, by force if necessary."

"I will do that," she replied softly, and she turned with what she hoped was queenly dignity and strode towards the hall. "Elene, take Higd back to my cambrai."

The hall was a scene of confusion. Trestles and benches were piled against the walls to make room for the arming of the warriors. Finn was in his chamber, surrounded by treasure. Warriors assigned to the door would remain at their posts throughout the proceedings, ready to kill in an instant anyone who dared attempt to enter that sacred space and steal even a portion of the enormous treasure. All around her men sharpened swords and battle axes on whetstones, donned leather corslets, and laced thick war boots that covered their feet and most of their legs. A few of the men looked up as she passed, and then bent their heads to their work again, not acknowledging the queen.

Hildeburh saw Raefn across the crowded room. She picked her way through the men towards her son. He was just thirteen, with long legs and big feet that betokened more growth. He will be taller than his father by the time he is finished, she thought. He still wore the sword with the raven hilt his father had given him six years before; one of the smiths had enlarged the blade and thickened the handle so it was now a sword for a young man, not a boy.

"My son," Hildeburh said gently as she came to his place. Other boys his age encircled him, all wanting to be the companions of the king's son. She had heard, in songs and from the women's gossip, that Raefn could be a fierce fighter; he had killed full grown men with his sword and had steered Finn's eagle-prowed ship in a beach landing the previous summer. The girls in Finnsburgh flirted outrageously before the prince, whose dark hair and flashing eyes would have earned him female attention even if he had not been royal. Hildeburh had seen him only twice that winter, from a distance, and now her heart ached as she saw how grown he was, and she realized she hardly knew him. She remembered the days before his monwart, when they had talked all day long, and he had told her stories, sang her songs, and detailed his dreams. She had no idea, now, if he even missed her. His defense of her last autumn had been wonderful, but she was not allowed to see him, even to thank him. Finn had made sure of that.

"Hello, Mother," Raefn replied pleasantly. "Don't worry about all this"—he swept his hand around the hall—"it's just a show to intimidate the Danes. No one will get hurt. Father will make them humble themselves, and then he will exact tribute and make peace."

"I was supposed to make that peace, my son, by my marriage before you were born. But the Danes were strong and battle-ready then, and now they are wracked by famine. Don't forget, Raefn, that they are your kin too."

Raefn looked at her calmly, and she saw in his eyes the eyes of a four year old who had just discovered that crayfish eat bugs. She bit her tongue to keep from crying. "My blood is my father's now, not yours. You know that," he said plainly.

"Your father will not let me greet my brother on the beach," she said.

"I'm sure he has his reasons, mother. Finn is a good and wise king, and he always does what is best for the tribe. Now go to your cambrai, mother; don't try to see him and argue with him about it. I am sure that in a little while Finn will send a message asking you to come to the hall to pass the cup at a feast celebrating the renewed peace alliance with the Danes." He smiled reassuringly. "And then you will see your brother and have news of your Danish kin."

She nodded and turned away, making her way slowly back through the hall. Raefn and Higd hardly knew each other, she reflected. They had no bond like she and Hnaef did. Seven years apart in age, Raefn had probably not seen his sister in almost a year. Years from now, Higd wouldn't care if her husband forbade her from greeting Raefn. Higd revered Raefn from afar, but she did not love him.

The door to the king's chamber opened as she passed, and Finn strode through, dressed in his finest war gear. His pearl-studded gold circlet fitted over his helmet, and jewel

encrusted plates protected his chest and back, hinged with
leather straps and fastened with silver buckles. On his belt
hung his axe, a war hammer, and his sword, its hilt set with
gems and carved with Oden's runes. His shield was slung
over his back, and his leather war boots were tipped with
iron spikes. His short black tunic barely covered his breech
wrappings. She saw Cyneheard behind him.

She stopped and inclined her head to her husband, who
scowled when he saw her. "I know what to do with you,"
he said fiercely, and he came towards her menacingly. She
held her ground, praying to Freyja that she would at least
see her brother before her husband killed her, for that was
surely his intent.

"What shall we do with this Danish baggage?" he
howled, and a shudder ran through her as she heard
the echoes of the howls of the Danish men during the
ceremony to Odin long ago, when the Danes were strong
and Hoc was king and she had never heard of Friesland. He
picked her up and threw her over his shoulder; her head
slammed against the wood of his shield, missing the iron
spike in the shield's center by a hand's width. Dizzy from
the blow and upside down, Hildeburh faded in and out of
consciousness as Finn carried her out of the hall.

He's going to kill me on the beach in front of Hnaef,
she thought, and then she blacked out into a vision of
Hnaef's body on the rock in Denmark when she cut off
his hand, but he was an adult, not a youth, and the rock

changed to a funeral pyre. She moaned and briefly regained consciousness to realize that her head was knocking onto Finn's shield with each step he took. She struggled briefly, enough to make him change his grip on her so she could hang weakly onto the shield and lessen the impact. Finn laughed, horribly, and struck her hard across the back of her thighs before throwing her to the ground.

The pain in her legs kept her from standing, and she looked around blearily. She was in her cambrai. "Don't leave this place, witch. As of now, all my men will have orders to kill you if they see you outside these walls. You will die just as the blue handed forest witches died long ago." She raised her swollen, bruised face to look at him. She could not speak.

"Oh yes, Cyneheard told me. But the secret is safe with me." He kicked her, almost as an afterthought, before he left, slamming the door behind him. She heard a thud and knew that he had bolted her in.

"Mama?" Higd's whisper came from under the bed. Hildeburh could not move.

"I'm here, Higd. I can't get up yet, but I'm here, and we are together. Finn has bolted the door, and we cannot leave."

Higd carefully crept out from under the featherbed. Her eyes were swollen and her cheeks puffy from crying. Scared and tired, the light blond liveliness that made Higd seem elfin had disappeared. She came over to her mother and huddled against her. Hildeburh wrapped an arm around her daughter. "We should sleep, sweetheart. It's been a terrible day. Rest will heal us and let us make some plans."

Soothed by her mother's words and embrace, Higd fell asleep almost immediately. Hildeburh felt her chest and abdomen grow warm from the little girl's body. She lay on the cold floorboards, dirty, bleeding, and aching, hugging her daughter and trying to decide what to do.

It was twilight when she awoke. Higd lay quietly, eyes open, waiting for her mother. Hildeburh's legs ached where Finn had struck her, but she thought she could stand. Her mouth felt thick, dry, caked with blood. Her left eye ached, and that side of her vision was blurred. She stood up and fought the wave of pain and nausea that washed over her.

"Higd, you will have to go for water. The door is barred, but we must have something to eat and drink." She staggered to the window and opened the wooden shutters that faced away from the hall and carefully lifted Higd and helped her through the small window space, passing a small water bag after her. "Go directly to the well, and then come back. Do not speak to anybody except Wealh or Elene, and if you see Wealh, ask her to come here if she can." Finn had reassigned Wealh to the kitchens in the fall, leaving Hildeburh to do all the work of her cambrai without any adult help. Higd nodded and hurried away towards the well, head down.

First I must feed us both and tend my injuries, she thought. *Next I have to think of a way to get us out of here—preferably on one of Hnaef's ships. If Finn hasn't killed Hnaef outright just because he felt like it,* she thought bitterly. She knew the overland route from Frisia to Denmark was long, dangerous, and difficult. She and Higd would never make it. She mentally reviewed all her stores of medicines and herbs, thinking about what she would pack and what she would have to leave behind. She had to have a bag ready to go. Maybe Finn would make her return part of the peace alliance. If there was a peace alliance.

The scene she viewed through the open shutter was still. All of the Frisians were in or near the hall, watching the excitement, knowing that their powerful king had nothing to fear from a ragged bunch of starving Danes. She saw Higd hurrying back from the well, the full bag slung over her shoulder, and was relieved to know that Finn was not going to take her daughter from her. At least not yet.

She helped Higd through the window and set about making a stew for them. Greens, dried meat, cut up tubers and carrots thickened with ground wheat would make a hearty meal for them and keep them sated for a long time. Hildeburh began making a tea to soothe the pain in her face and legs as Higd stirred the stew.

"Did you see Wealh?" she asked lightly, not wanting to alarm her daughter.

"No, I didn't see anybody. There was a lot of noise over by the hall, but no one was at the well." They worked in silence for a while. Then, "Mama, what will happen to us?"

"I don't know, Higd, but the goddess will keep us, no matter what. Promise me, my daughter, that if Finn kills me, you will always remember that I love you more than anything on this earth," she said tensely. Higd nodded solemnly, her eyes brimming with tears. Might as well prepare her for it now, Hildeburh thought grimly.

"Queen," Hildeburh heard a whisper at the window. It was Elene. She looked out.

"Elene—you shouldn't be here." Aescher and Lyda would want Elene to stay away from Hildeburh more than ever now.

"No one misses me. They're all in the hall, watching Hnaef Half-Hand humble himself before Finn. The winter was hard on your people, Queen, and the Dane offers only two boats and wants only food in return at the end of the summer."

"Who is with him?" Eagerness for news of her people overrode Hildeburh's sense of caution.

"A bard with dark skin and white hair, who is painfully thin and yet carries a beautiful carved harp as well as his sword and shield. The other Dane is shorter and plain looking, older than the bard and the king, and he wears a White Christ necklace over his byrnie." Bjorn and Hengest, Hildeburh thought. My brother has good counsel if nothing else.

"Finn hasn't called for food yet, and he is giving the Danes mead so they will be quickly drunken in their famine-starved bodies. He wants Hnaef to pledge fealty and make Finn High King of Denmark and then to swear allegiance to Edgtheow and the Jutes as well. Hnaef may soon be drunk enough to do it."

Hildeburh stared into the darkening dusk of west Finnsburgh. Her brother was only a short walk from her, yet she would not see him as he bargained for his own life and the life of his people, perhaps even her life. "Has Hnaef asked for me, Elene?" She kept her voice steady.

"Yes, Queen, and Finn put him off, saying you were ill. I could tell that this did not satisfy him, but he is in no position to argue. Cynna sits by Finn's throne, my Lady, and all the women and warriors know that you are locked in here."

"Where is Wealh?"

"I don't know—probably in the kitchen."

"Has Hnaef mentioned my mother, Freawaru, Hoc's queen?"

"She survived the winter, my Lady, but many of the old people did not. Hnaef is king of only about forty people right now, he said. Finn talked of sending him back to

Denmark and having the remnants of the Danes move here."

Sending him back? That made no sense. Equinox was almost here, Edgtheow and the other client kings would arrive any day now with their war bands, and the whole fleet would travel together through the summer, raiding the Angles, the Eirans, the Mercians.

Hildeburh thought fast. If Finn made Hnaef and the Danes leave, it could only mean that they would not be in the viking fleet. And if they weren't in the fleet, they were enemies. Finn intended to let the Danes go, then chase them down and kill them. They were worthless to him as allies; better to kill the men and round up the remaining women and children—if there were any children left alive—to sell as slaves.

"Elene," she said urgently. "You must get a message to my brother for me." She thought quickly. If Elene were caught betraying her people, her father himself would kill her instantly. She couched the message in terms Elene couldn't understand. "You probably won't be able to get near Hnaef, but Bjorn—the bard—or Hengest—the warrior with the Christ token—will listen if you give them a message from me. Tell them that Finn plans what Hoc did to the Geats when I was thirteen. And tell them that the old men ride the sea in the back, waiting for victory."

Elene looked puzzled, but she repeated the message three times until Hildeburh was satisfied she knew it and then sent her off.

The dusk had turned into darkness by the time Hildeburh and Higd ate their stew and settled down for the night. "What will happen, Mama?" Higd asked again as they settled into the featherbed together and Hildeburh sighed with relief as her aching body sank into the softness.

"I don't know, sweetheart." Hildeburh could see the inside of her cambrai in the glow of the embers of the fire, could see the weavings lining the walls and the pots and baskets she had made. A new smock for Higd was on the loom, and her herbs and medicines carefully stored in their leather bags. The dowry chests were full of children's clothes and toys; Finn had taken her jewels back long ago. She missed only the circlet with the pearls and rubies, for it reminded her of the time early in her marriage when she had liked Finn and had hoped they would be happy together.

"Your father wants me to stay in here, and you and Elene can fetch water and food, if we need it, and we'll see what happens. The king must decide what he wants to do with us, Higd, and until he does, we will stay here and eat and tell stories and sing songs. I will show you how to finish weaving your new smock, and we will sew it together when it comes off the loom. Does that sound good?"

But Higd was already asleep, lulled by the sound of her mother's voice making ordinary plans about chores as if the day had not been full of horror.

Three days later, Hildeburh had not left her cambrai. No one paid any attention to her, and Higd had gone to the well for water and emptied the basket of waste each day. No one had spoken to her as she left the cambrai through the window; there seemed to be a tacit agreement among the tribe that as long as the door bolt remained in place and Hildeburh did not leave the cambrai, Higd was free to do errands. Elene had not returned. Wealh was nowhere to be seen.

Very early in the morning of the third day, Hildeburh was awakened by a scratching sound at the shutter. She slipped out of bed without awakening Higd and peeked thorough the shutter. It was Elene, who looked ghostly in her white smock in the gloom of early dawn.

"Queen," she said.

"Elene." Hildeburh slipped an arm through the window to give Elene a partial embrace. "Are you safe here?"

"My family is still asleep. And I miss you, Queen."

"I miss you too, Elene, and I miss roaming the forests and the beaches with you and Higd. What news from the hall? Has Finn said he will release me and Higd to Hnaef?"

"The Danes left two days ago," Elene said. It was as Hildeburh feared, then. They were not to be in the viking fleet. "And now Finn talks of giving Raefn his first real command and letting him attack Hnaef instead of making the Danes into clients. I gave the bard your message, Queen. I stopped him on his way to the latrine pit and told him your words."

"What did he say?"

"Nothing at first. Then he muttered something about you being thirteen, and his eyes darkened. I was scared, Queen, and then he looked almost as if he would cry, and he asked me where you were, and how you fared, and I told you were locked in your cambrai with only your daughter, and he got angrier still."

"Yes. And then what?"

"That was all, Queen. And now I must go. My mother will want me."

"Do you still say the prayer to Freyja every morning and every night, Elene?"

"Oh, yes."

"Goddess bless you, child. Come back with more news when you can." Hildeburh watched the girl disappear into the early morning gloom. The birds had just started their chatter.

It was the magic day of springtime, she reflected. *The day and night are equal today, a good day for visions and magic. But I don't want to see the future*, she thought, and she kept her mind firmly on her work as she set about getting some breakfast ready. She and Higd would spend the day weaving. Each day, Higd was spending more and more time outside as she went to fetch water, and Hildeburh couldn't blame her. The four walls of the cambrai seemed closer together every day. They both slept a lot, from boredom as well as exhaustion, and Hildeburh's injuries were almost healed.

Later that morning, Hildeburh watched through the front shutter as the Frisian warriors and the client warbands made their way towards the hall. Mead-drinking preceded the rituals of Woden, and then there would be a feast before the next day's departure. Finn usually handed out weapons at the feast of spring equinox, making clear his expectations for the warriors' war-work that coming season.

At midday, the shouts and cheers from the hall were loud enough for Hildeburh to hear them. Higd had gone to the well with strict instructions to be back before the men left for Woden's island in the harbor—Hildeburh didn't want Finn to see or think about Higd in his violent drunkenness before his bloody ceremonies.

Higd had not yet returned, and the sun was almost at its midpoint. Hildeburh felt knots in her stomach and in the back of her neck. Don't let him see her, goddess, she prayed. Let her come safe to me, and this summer when the men are gone, Higd and I will escape. We will take the overland route and live in the forest and find a tribe that will welcome my healing skills, and we will live out our days together with an inland people that has never heard of Finn.

Hildeburh had repeated this story to herself many times this morning, having realized that since Hnaef had gone, he was as good as dead, and Hoc's frithstowe wouldn't exist much longer. With infinite sadness, she had discarded her dreams of returning to Denmark. She would never see her mother or brother or Sunya again.

The men were leaving the hall. Hide, Higd. Duck behind a corner, and stay there until they're on the beach. Don't try to run for it. Higd was wise for her age. She would figure it out, Hildeburh reassured herself. They would file out the main entrance and go to the beach. They wouldn't see her.

She looked out the half-open shutter at the back of the hall, listening and imagining what was happening on the other side. But then the sound changed direction, and Hildeburh realized that the men were coming around the hall, towards her. She quickly closed the shutter all the way so she could peer out through the slats, but they would not be able to look from the bright daylight into the cambrai's shadows and see her.

The main part of the Frisian warband came around the corner of the hall. Finn, Cyneheard, Raefn, Aescher, and Handschue led the others. Hildeburh could tell they had been drinking heavily. They stopped in front of her cambrai.

They have come for me, she thought. That was his plan all along. To sacrifice me to his war god. She felt only anger, not fear, and relief that Higd was not there to watch.

But instead, Finn turned to the men behind him. "Bring me Wealh, the former slave of the Dane, who now works in the kitchens," he said. Moments later they were back, holding Wealh between them by her elbows. She stood as tall as the warriors, and even from a distance Hildeburh could see the Moon Goddess tattoo on Wealh's big, bare foot. Will they force her to get me ready for the sacrifice? she wondered dispassionately.

Cyneheard took a leather thong and bound it around Wealh's neck. The men released her arms. One opened her mouth and held it open as she struggled, and Cyneheard poured some liquid into her mouth from the flask at his belt, and Hildeburh realized, with a jolt, that Wealh was to be the sacrifice, not her. Finn just wanted her to know.

Knowing she could do nothing, Hildeburh prayed to Freyja and to Wealh's Moon Goddess, who were really one, that Wealh might have an easy death and find her ancestors in the spirit world of the garden. Wealh closed her eyes as the magic took effect, and she stumbled along the path unseeing, pulled like an animal on a leash. The group made its way to the beach. Wealh's bones would join those of the other women killed on that island to give glory to Woden and Finn and fighting and death. Hildeburh dug her nails into her palms, hating the warriors and their gods and their rituals. Higd, she thought. Higd will be back soon.

Chapter Ten

The summer began, and Hildeburh found herself more and more alone in the hot, dark cambrai. Higd scrambled out the window in the mornings right after eating and often didn't return until midday, full of stories of her explorations and chores with other girls her age. Hildeburh's loneliness was dismal and depressing, but despite a sense of resentment at her daughter's absences, she was relieved that Higd had achieved some sort of normal routine.

Freyja's garden lay in a shambles behind the cambrai. Weeds choked the young plants that had returned on their own, and the vines spilled into the radiating spokes of the walkways. Hildeburh tried not to brood on the destruction and the bleak prospect of the winter ahead, if they were still here, when she would have to send Higd to beg for food in the kitchens.

She planned to flee at midsummer, when the women and children would feast with the priests of Frey in the hall. She and Higd would hurry through the compound, food and clothes and medicines strapped to Hildeburh's back, and they would slip through the back gate and up into the forest. Elene had told her that Edgwold, Cyneheard's apprentice, and Guthlac, an older man whose son had just joined Aescher's crew, were priests of Frey for the summer. Neither of them was skilled in tracking or hunting, and Hildeburh hoped to travel most of the midsummer night—the moon would be full—and into the next morning before their escape was discovered.

She practiced walking rapidly in circles in the cambrai with her largest water bag slung over her shoulders. She stood straight, then squatted as deeply as she could and forced herself upright again, clenching her teeth against the weight of the full bag. I must be strong, she told herself, or we will never make it.

The moon was just three days away from full when Hildeburh was awakened from a midday doze by shouts of excitement and turmoil. She looked out her window, open almost all the time now, as the Frisian women hurried to the beach. The lookouts shouted reports of eagle-prowed ships in the harbor. Finn was back, in the middle of the season, with the whole fleet.

It seemed like hours that Hildeburh stood by the window, wishing she could get news of the landing. Higd had been sensible enough to come straight back to her mother's cambrai when the alarm had first sounded, and she now slept soundly on the featherbed, worn out from a morning spent playing in the sun. The parts of the frithstowe that Hildeburh could see remained deserted.

Then the wind from the harbor blew the sounds of voices towards her; she could tell that a large party was making its way towards the hall. She closed her front shutter almost all the way and peered through the remaining slit.

Finn and Aescher came around the corner of the hall. Finn's left arm hung in a sling, and Aescher wore a bandage around his head. *They have had battle trouble*, she thought, pleased to see that her husband was not as invincible as he thought he was. Then she noticed the two figures walking behind him, and her stomach clenched as she recognized Bjorn and Hengest, dressed in crude war-gear but carrying fine swords.

She drew back towards the hearth, quickly covering Higd's sleeping form with a light cloth; her daughter looked like part of the bedclothes. The bolt on her door slid back heavily. It had not moved for three months.

Finn opened the door without looking into the cambrai. "She's in there," he said. "Be in the hall for the feast when the sun goes below the trees." He and Aescher left.

Hengest and Bjorn stood awkwardly in the door frame, peering into the darkness. Hildeburh stepped forward.

"My people," she said, her voice and her hands shaking, "my kin. I welcome you in sorrow to Friesland." Before she fully knew what she was doing, she was touching them, their arms, their shoulders, crying and sobbing. "Where is my brother? Can I leave with you? Why are you here at midsummer?"

"Peace, my Lady," Hengest said gently. Then, more formally, "Even in the midst of our troubles, I rejoice to see Hildeburh, daughter of Hoc, childhood friend of my beloved wife."

"How does Sunya?"

"She was well in Denmark when I left her, Queen, and hope she still is. She does not believe in the White Christ as I do, but I know he watches over her even so. But now we must talk to you, and tell you what has happened, so you can join with us in counsel as we try to save the Scyldings."

Hildeburh's heart lightened. These were her people, not Finn's, and they valued and sought her counsel.

"Bjorn will tell you all. He has been our bard since Caedmon's passing and knows better than I how to put a tale of important events together."

Bjorn looked at Hildeburh, and she wondered what he saw. She knew her hair was partly grey now, after twenty nine winters, and her wide hips and fleshy stomach showed her childbearing. His eyes betrayed nothing, however, as he began to speak.

"Just before the equinox, we came to Frisia to parley in the two boats we still sailed. Times have been hard in Denmark, Hildeburh, even before Hoc died, and some of the Scyldings whispered it was the curse of the goddess for his theft of her acolyte. Crops failed; ponies fell sick and died; and summer takings grew fewer and less rich. Last fall we had only a little food—all of us would have died. Hnaef had already traded almost everything we had for food—tapestries, extra armor, even cook pots, and baskets. So we sailed to Jutland and raided their storerooms. It was a choice between plundering food or starving, and we chose plundering.

"So we broke the alliance with the Jutes and angered Finn. We knew it but didn't have the time before winter locked in to come here and promise amends." Hildeburh nodded.

"You know we were here in the spring. Finn ordered us to gather our women and children and anything worth taking and return to Finnsburgh before the spring rites of Odin—all in two or three days. He knew, of course, that it was impossible. When Hnaef tried to suggest we stay and collect the rest of the tribe at the end of the summer, Finn sent him off. So we knew we were not truly in an alliance with Finn, even though he said we were."

Hildeburh had to admire her husband's deviousness. He kept his honor intact by not killing the Danes in his hall, and yet he could increase his honor later in the summer by saying that the Danes had not returned in the time agreed upon, so the peace agreement was forfeit, and he was glorified in killing the perfidious traitors who did not keep their word.

"But the second half of your message, my Lady, was news to us, and we thank you. Hoc always scattered the older men throughout the fleet so that their wisdom and experience would balance the younger men's strength and inexperience. We had no idea that the grey-haired Frisians hung to the back as easy targets for clever warriors.

"Finn took his time catching up to us, maybe because he enjoyed the thought of us dreading his advance. He seems to enjoy his enemies' distress overmuch." Hildeburh silently nodded. "We had to break a lot too—we had no food and no wind, and famine-thinned arms cannot row for long periods.

"When we arrived at the mouth of the Scylding harbor, we finally sighted Finn's ships behind us. We ducked into upper north cove—with only two boats, it was easy to hide. As Finn's ships entered the harbor, we heard the lookouts sound the alarm and knew the women and children would be making their way to the caves in the forest." Bjorn had been gazing blankly at the wall before him as he told the events of the early summer; Hengest nodded occasionally and murmured his agreement. Then he looked directly at Hildeburh, and she wanted to weep when she saw the despair and pain in his eyes, and she knew suddenly that Hnaef was dead, that was why he had not come with them, and Bjorn dreaded telling her.

"A boatload of old men did indeed remain at the mouth of the harbor. The harbor itself was jammed with Finn's ships and the ships of his allies. We could hear their howls of rage and disappointment when they found nothing but a dilapidated hall and some ramshackle outbuildings. The Danes are not prosperous now, Lady, and there was nothing to take. They made a brief search for the remaining people but were soon back in the ships, and we could hear Finn's voice issuing orders about reforming the fleet and killing the Danes on sight.

"I didn't know exactly what Hnaef had planned. I was sure we would all die with no glory since none but Frisian bards would ever sing our deaths. But I was ready to kill warriors of the tribe that dishonored and imprisoned you, my Lady, and to die defending your honor that way."

Hildeburh must have shown her surprise, for Bjorn continued, "You have always been the princess I loved with all my heart and spirit, Hildeburh, and I have never taken a wife. By the time my youthful anger at you had faded, your father had sent you away, but I would have honored Finn had he honored you as you deserve." Hengest shifted uneasily in his place where he stood by the fire. Bjorn continued.

"We advanced on the ship full of old men. Amidships sat a greybeard with a crutch and only one leg; he was singing a battle song of Folcwalda's battle with Hoc, and I could see from the runes on his cloak that he was Finn's bard.

"He saw us, coming at them through the mist, and broke off the song to sound the alarm. But the noise from the main harbor deafened the Frisian warriors, and we killed the greybeards with ease, replacing our crude weapons with their fine swords." He gestured briefly to the weapon that leaned against the wall, fine steel with runes carved directly into the blade; it was Cyneheard's old sword, and the gems at the base of the hilt had been his reward for the loss of his leg in the service of Folcwalda.

"Cyneheard the Bard caused me much pain in my time in Finnsburgh, Bjorn Hunlafing. I am glad to hear that he walks in the spirit world now." Even though Cyneheard had already told Finn about Gefean, maybe the loss of the spiteful old bard would make Finn more amenable to letting her return to Denmark.

"Hnaef Half-Hand showed wisdom and courage in what followed, Lady. Finn's ship was leading the way out of Scylding harbor when Finn's lookout saw us and realized what had happened. He sounded the attack, and they charged us. The eagle came towards us, and fire arrows fell out of the sky from the boats at Finn's rear. The mass of ships filled the neck of the harbor, and in that narrow space it was as if we fought only two or three ships rather than the twenty or thirty that Finn now commands. Finn himself rose on the front bench of his ship, and as soon as I saw him I hurled a war-hammer his way. It struck him on the left elbow, not his head, as I'd intended, and he screamed, more in anger than pain. I don't think Finn, King of the Northern and Western Seas, has had a war wound in many summers.

"But he stood straight, with his left arm limp, and picked up a spear in his right hand. He hurled the battle-spear, fine ash and straight, toward your brother as he stood amidships, guiding his rowers. We Danes thought only to cut down as many of the enemy as we could before their numbers and their well-fed sword arms overcame us.

"The spear entered deep, and pierced Hnaef's belly—he had traded his byrnie for food last spring. It lodged there, and I knew immediately that if I pulled it out, it would simply make the blood gush and bring his death more quickly. In the odd silence of the noise of battle, I heard a rasping sound as the life-blood oozed and the spirit started to drain from my king's body. Hnaef wore no circlet, for all our treasure had been traded, but he stood tall and kingly, and he advanced to the bow and leaned upon the dragon head of the boat that was his, that had been his father's, and he threw his sword into the sea to show that he wished to speak before he died.

"It is an old custom, among warriors, to let a dying king speak in the midst of battle, and to remember his words." Hildeburh nodded; she knew stories of such customs but had doubted such things actually happened. "He pointed to Finn and swept his arm around, showing the company the harbor that had been his. He said, 'You allies of Finn who fight here with him against this ragged band of starving warriors, beware this lord who pledges what he wishes and breaks his pledges when he pleases. He tasked us impossibly so he could kill us, we who had been allies so noble that he married our princess, my sister, to protect himself from my father, our king. You Jutes and Eiders and Saxons, beware, for now you are in his favor and have his pledge, but my death and my sister's captivity show that he is not a warrior of honor, not a prince who keeps his pledges, and you cannot trust this lord to keep his alliance with you. I die here in my own harbor, my honor complete, and I wish to you, fellow client-kings of Finn, that such a glorious end may find you someday, but Finn is a snake and a trickster, and you may not...'

"An arrow finished him, then, Lady, shot from the eagle-ship of Finn by a warrior raging at the insults to his king. It went into his throat. I shot back with a bow and arrow I had taken from the old men's boat, and we heard the thud as it hit one of Finn's crewmen.

"Lady," Bjorn stopped his tale. Hildeburh had gone white, and her jawline was tinged with green as she thought about an arrow entering Hnaef's throat, cutting off his speech as he revealed Finn's true nature to the rest of the allies. She couldn't stop herself from imagining the blood running down his throat as the pain in his neck mingled with the pain in his abdomen before the blackness closed in.

"Lady, there's more, and we haven't much more time. We can grieve for our king later." She nodded.

"A cry arose from Finn's ship. 'The prince has been hit,' a warrior shouted, and Finn....Lady? Hildeburh?"

"My son. Is he dead?" It had never crossed her mind to worry about Raefn's safety. He had seemed to share Finn's invincibility.

"Yes, Lady. The arrow felled him, and he died not long after. Finn is crazed with grief for his son and lusts for my death in revenge. Edgtheow, the Jute, and Aescher, Finn's second, urged him to call parley rather than to kill us all then and there, although he wanted only battle. I think Hnaef's last words made a great impact upon the other client kings, and if they ever trusted Finn, they surely do not now. Finn wants us dead, but his advisors insist he honor the peace and not be known as a peace-breaker.

"So we have come to Finnsburgh at midsummer and tonight will bargain for our lives in the great hall, and we need your counsel, Lady, in the wake of the deaths of your son and brother, and we need your guidance for the future of the Danes."

"I will grieve later, as you say, for the sun is almost below the trees." Hildeburh felt an emptiness in her very soul and knew that it would be there until the day she died. Her eldest child was dead, killed in battle by a man who still loved her, if not in the way he had when they were young. She thought for some time, staring into the depths of the fire, willing the wisdom of the goddess to come to her. An ember snapped, the sound deafening in the silent cambrai, and she suddenly realized the solution.

"My counsel is this, kinsmen. I will go to the hall with you and ask my husband for a joint funeral for Hnaef and Raefn. This funeral will be the start of a new peace, a fresh peace, that will take the place of the peace I was supposed to pledge in my marriage, that will take the place of the false peace you bargained earlier this past spring. The remnants of the Danes will go on viking journey with Finn for the remainder of the season. They will receive plunder as well as food like any honored ally. At the end of the summer, the Frisian princess Higd and I will accompany you back to Denmark. She will pledge peace to a Danish youth, and when they are both of age, they will marry. Until that time, Hengest will be Finn's deputy in Denmark—it cannot be Bjorn, for he is the killer of the Frisian prince. Higd's first son will be named Raefn, and he will be client king in Denmark to Finn's successor here. Finn's grandchildren will rule Denmark, and his honor will be sated."

"That might satisfy him," Hengest said slowly. "We will lay this plan before him and see if he agrees." They all rose to make their way to the hall.

"I have something for you, Queen, that might give you strength for the coming parley," Hengest said. "Before I left my home and my wife this spring, she told me that I should give this to you when I saw you." He opened the pouch attached to the side of his tunic and rummaged through it. "We thought, of course, that I would see you in the spring, for we had no idea that Finn would go so far as to keep you from seeing your kin and people." He drew from his pouch the necklace pendant of Freyja that Bruna had given to Sunya twenty summers before. It hung on a rough cord of horsehair; Freyja's wide bottom and large breasts were worn smooth from years of gently rubbing on Sunya's throat.

"Thank you, kinsman," Hildeburh said simply and hung it around her neck. It would be her only ornament when she entered the hall.

She crossed the room to her bed and lifted the light blanket. Higd lay under it, eyes wide open. "Can I come out, Mama? Is it safe? And why is my brother dead? Who are these men?" Hildeburh smiled in spite of her grief and the danger all around.

Higd shrank close to her mother when Hengest and Bjorn began to laugh at her breathless questions, but she did not protest when Bjorn reached over and picked her up. She looked at him solemnly with quiet fear in her eyes.

"She looks like you, Queen, and will make a fine Danish queen some day. We must go and make that peace, so we can bring this fairy child back to our homeland."

"Higd, don't get into mischief. There are oatcakes in the hearth and water in the bag. Don't go too far. I'll be back later tonight. And don't repeat whatever parts of this talk you might have heard," she said sternly before she left the cambrai with the Danes.

The cool late afternoon air felt delicious. "I have not left those walls since the day you arrived here in Frisia last spring," she remarked as they made their way around the hall to the main entrance. She hoped the gentleness of the air would influence her husband's feelings towards the Danish proposal.

That night was like the night of the double funeral, two days later. The full moon reminded Hildeburh of her plans for escape that night, the plans that she had abandoned with the arrival of Bjorn and Hengest and the chance for a renewed life in Denmark. She walked between her tribesmen as they made their way toward the North Hill, leading the warriors who bore Hnaef's body. Before them walked the Danes bearing Raefn. Finn headed the whole procession, grim and silent. In the warm air he sweated under the weight of his gold circlet and torque, but like the rest of the Frisians and Danes, Finn was there to grieve and give to the fallen.

In the numbness of her grief, Hildeburh felt also her own surprise at Finn's ready acquiescence to her plan of peace. Aescher and Handschue had urged him to accept, so not to sully his honor by breaking his word, even to a people as powerless as the Danes. In the days since the abrupt return of the fleet, Finn had done little but drink mead, passing out in the hall only to wake and start drinking again.

Now he led the procession as they reached the bottom of the hill. Hildeburh could see him straining at the climb and knew the days of drinking and grief were taking their toll. His circlet gleamed in the moonlight and in the light of the torches that lined the funerary route from hall to hill.

He stopped at the large double grave that the slaves had dug that day. It was full of kindling and dried logs. Two reed mats were suspended over the grave, tied onto stakes at the edges. He gestured to his men, who carefully lowered Raefn's body onto one of the mats.

The noises struck Hildeburh more than anything, and she thought that in coming years she would remember most clearly the sound of the funeral. She heard the sounds of the night, the keening of insects and the whirring of owls, the popping of the burning torches and the faint clanking sounds of arm-rings banging together as the warriors led their princes to their final rest. Gravel crunched underfoot, and breathing seemed loud. But nobody spoke, and there was no music, as the group ranged itself along the grave.

Raefn had been dressed in his finest war gear over the soft wool tunic she had made for him the summer before. Finn had carefully placed the silver circlet on his dead son's head and wrapped the cold and stiffened fingers around the raven-sword hilt as best he could. Raefn's shield covered his torso, masking the arrow wound that had killed him. His helmet, adorned with a boar's head and inlaid with golden runes, was tucked under his left arm.

Finn removed his thickest gold arm-ring, encrusted with pearls and amethysts cut to glitter in the torchlight. "My son," he said strongly, his voice still loud and commanding despite the days spent drinking and grieving, "take this to Valhalla to present to our Lord Woden All-Father. It shows your worth as a prince, as a thane, as a warrior. You were a fierce fighter, a wise counselor, a valiant leader, and a crafty hunter. You would have followed me as king of the Western and Northern Seas. Now I shall not see you again, my only living blood, until we meet in Valhalla. Goodbye, my noble prince and son." He placed the arm-ring in the center of Raefn's shield and stepped back.

Bjorn and Hengest held Hnaef's shoulders and, with the help of Guthlaf and Oslaf, placed Hnaef's body on the other mat. Uncle and nephew lay together in death, Hnaef's tunic plain and worn next to the splendid funeral raiment of his sister's son. A strip of cloth hid his mangled throat; a crude shield lay over his torso, covering the wound of the spear that had ripped apart his guts.

Hengest stepped forward as Finn had, intending to speak at the funeral of his king, but Hildeburh suddenly moved to the front of the group and then gently pushed him back. "Hnaef was my brother," she said firmly, "and I must bid him farewell as his only kin here." Hengest nodded.

She looked down at the corpses before her, her beautiful dark-haired son looking richly peaceful in death, the grey in her brother's tawny hair and the deep set lines around his eyes showing the strain of the brief years of his kingship. "Hnaef Half-Hand, King of the Danes for just ten summers, has left us to walk in the spirit world. He died king of a famished, weakened people—none can deny it. But he also died king of a loyal warband, king of honor and dignity and strength. I dreamed of a kings' friendship between my brother and my son, not a meeting in death and warrior's grief, but my son could find no better companion on his way to the world of the dead." She looked fiercely at Finn. "Hnaef was honorable, strong, and courageous. He protected his people as best he could, and his tribe revered him. He lost half his hand defending our father, the noble Hoc, and has now lost his life defending his people.

"These deaths make a black peace for these tribes. Woe to the one who breaks it." She knelt in the dust at the side of the pit. As Finn had given Raefn the arm-ring, she must give Hnaef a token, yet she had nothing. The goddess necklace that still hung around her throat was not a fitting adornment for a fallen warrior. She had insisted that none of the Danes give up his weapons to burn with their king; the warriors would need their swords and other battle gear as they journeyed with Finn during the remainder of the summer.

"My token to mark your passing, brother, is not gold or jewels or rich weaponry. As many years ago I cut off your hand to save your life, today I cut off my hair to mark your death."

From her pocket she removed her knife, sharpened that morning on a whetstone for just this use, and uncoiled the long thick braid that usually was tucked and wrapped neatly at the nape of her neck. Unbraided, her dark hair, riddled with grey, reached to her thighs. She unsheathed the blade and sliced through the braid at its beginning, leaving her hair hanging freely around her shoulders. She draped the hair diagonally over her brother's body so that part of it gently brushed his face.

"You have a token of your sister's and your people's love as you journey in death, my brother. Meet our noble father there, and greet him for me as you tell him how you passed to the afterlife." She rose and nodded to the torchbearers, who handed a torch to her and one to Finn.

For the first time in many years, Finn and Hildeburh stood side by side joined in a common enterprise, and the loss of her marriage cut her deeply as she stood before the pyre of her other losses, her son, her brother. Together they thrust the lighted torches under the suspended mats into the grave, and the growing crackling and the low roar told them that the fire had caught.

Under the sound of the flames, she said quietly to Finn, "My Lord, if nothing else, we can grieve together, for we both loved him dearly."

Finn looked at her with his red rimmed eyes full of hate. "Peace or no, I will not forget that my only son was killed by a Dane." Then he turned and began the climb back down to Finnsburgh. Most of the Frisians followed him.

Hildeburh turned to the slaves. "I will tend the fire. You go back to your regular duties." And as if she were still queen, they obeyed.

The Danes ranged behind her, reclining on the hill. There were only seventeen of them, and she had met each in the past two days, remembering childhood friendships and family ties. Some of the warriors were so young that Hildeburh had helped at their births, and they had smiled with pleasure as she praised and remembered their mothers and fathers, mostly dead now from the years of famine and weakness.

The fire was eating away at the reed mats, already scorched black from the heat. Raefn's caught first—it was heavier, loaded with weapons and gold, and hung lower in the pit—then the flames spread to Hnaef's, and the bodies crashed into the pit at almost the same time. Hildeburh watched as her hair and Hnaef's shrank and curled and finally disintegrated in the flames. She watched the gold of the arm ring on Raefn's shield melt, and she smelled the putrid, burnt flesh, the smell masked somewhat by the scent of burning flower petals that had been packed around the logs.

She reached up to caress the figure of Freyja around her neck. She had found that absentmindedly stroking the smooth figurine calmed her and helped her think, and she believed that the wisdom and serenity of the goddess flowed from the necklace to her. *Goddess*, she thought, *let their deaths not be in vain. Let the peace be honored so I can go back to Scyldingland and be your priestess once again. Let the growth of peacetime come so that no more mothers must watch their children burn or starve.*

The fire danced before her eyes as she stroked the pendant, and as the edges of her vision began to blur, she realized she was going into a trance of the goddess. She welcomed it, yearning towards the mystical journey she had not found for so long. "Taste the flower and the fruit, see the flower and the fruit, smell the flower and the fruit," she whispered to herself, recalling suddenly the day of her girlhood when Bruna had taught her to trance. The fire melted into sunshine, and she was in Freyja's summer garden, dizzy with the scent of blossoms. She sensed rather than clearly saw fields full of ripening grain and knew that fruit and flowers grew in a profusion of plenty with the goddess' blessing. Far beyond, Hildeburh could just see ponies racing along the cliffs overlooking a rocky shore. She heard faint music that sounded like Higd and Elene singing to the goddess in their bell-like child's voices, and she heard also the songs of birds and the chatter of insects and frogs.

The music grew louder and closer, and she saw a procession through the trees to the garden's clearing in the mystical forest. At its head trotted the white elk, majestic and beautiful with a garland of full summer flowers draped around her neck. Her short horns and her hoofs were gold. Behind her came a flock of blue-handed women and girls, holding spindles and shuttles, banging them together to mark the rhythm of their passing.

In the center of the group were two pregnant women, assisted by their companions. Their enormous bellies showed that they were at their time, and their smocks were wet at the front where their milk was already running. They labored in tandem, and as a contraction surged through them both, the song of the women changed to a chant of frantic ecstasy in anticipation of the births.

The procession moved through the glade into the depths of the forest, and she sighed with longing as they departed. Someday she would come to Freyja's world and never leave and spend eternity in the garden of the goddess with its beauty and its rituals of birth and growth. But her time had not yet come.

Thoughts of her people and her duty ended her vision, but slowly, so that the mystical forest and the pyre before her mingled as the two worlds collided in her spirit. Gradually the ashes and the embers in the grave pit took on more substance until she realized that the pyre had almost burnt itself out, and soon it would be time to fill in the grave, cover the ashes of her son and brother and their tokens.

Behind her most of the Scyldings slept. Their camp on the beach by their boats was no different from the hillside—they still slept on the ground in their clothes—and as a group they had not wanted to go far from Hildeburh during their stay. She felt that they were anxious and wanted to keep her safe, but also that her presence reassured them that there was hope of a future for the Danes.

Some of the younger ones may become like sons to me, she thought ruefully. *Their mothers are dead, as is my son. I can be a mother to my people, though my childbearing days are over*. She and Hengest both knew that her counsel would make many of the decisions in the frithstowe upon their return. Through her grief, Hildeburh was excited at the prospect of returning and making Denmark strong and healthy again. She would be priestess, healer, and birther; with Sunya she would direct the care of the fields and the livestock. The women would weave and make baskets for trading, for Hengest said that more and more trading markets were opening as powerful kings like Finn made peace alliances and stopped the constant fighting in the Inner Sea. "The moon has set, my Lady, and our tribesmen are asleep," Bjorn's voice came softly out of the darkness behind her. "I have watched over you in your trance and wish you would share with me what you saw."

She turned and made out the dim outline of the bard leaning against a boulder a few feet away. His white-yellow hair gleamed in the faint starlight. She sat down next to him.

"The goddess welcomes Hnaef and Raefn into her spirit world. It is beautiful and peaceful there in that garden in the forest. Sometimes I long to go there and never return to this world of pain and feud."

Bjorn unwrapped his cloak from around himself and put his arms around her, wrapping her into the warmth of the rough cloak and the strength of his sinewy arms. She put her face against his chest and began to weep as he kissed her hair and rocked her as if she were a small child. She cried until she fell asleep in his arms, knowing he would stay awake until the departure of the fleet at sunrise.

Chapter Eleven

Hildeburh trudged to the hall in the chill spring afternoon, huddling into her thin cloak and rubbing her hands together to drive away the damp cold that refused to leave Friesland even after the long winter was supposed to be over.

It had been long, unbearably long, Hildeburh reflected as she passed through the main doors to look down the length of the hall to Finn's gift throne. The cold had kept Finn from carrying out his plans for expanding the hall, and the Frisians and the client warbands packed the hall, some spilling out the side door and the main doors to drink in the cold where there was room to stretch out.

The winter had ruined all their plans. The warriors had returned just before the autumnal equinox, their ships full of plunder and tribute. Hengest had led the Danes well, protecting Finn's flank and halting at least two ambushes, one from the Geatish king Hygelac, who refused to become a client king of Finn's. Finn had distributed the summer's treasures, keeping some but rewarding his thanes and followers and clients with the bulk of it.

The cold autumn had turned into winter overnight, and the day after the equinox the first of the blinding snows had fallen. Only three of the client kings had managed to ship out; Hengest and the others found the harbor locked in ice overnight, its entrance invisible in the blinding snow. The livestock and seed that Finn had bestowed upon them would have to wait until spring.

In the long winter afternoons and nights, Hengest and Bjorn and Hildeburh calculated over and over the time they would need to sail to Scyldingland, drop off the supplies with Hildeburh and Higd, and return to sail with Finn. They agonized over the twelve women and children left in Denmark with almost no food and no news, not knowing whether the scanty Danish warband still existed.

Hildeburh walked the length of the hall toward the empty throne, noting the tension and excitement of the men. They would be off soon—Finn would issue boarding orders at the feast, they were all sure—after a long winter cooped up in Finnsburgh. Finn had been enraged at the thought of having 260 uninvited guests for six months, but eventually resigned himself to it, sending the men hunting when he could, setting them to clearing snow when there was nothing else to do.

The snow had soon reached over the top of Higd's head, even though she had sprouted up as she approached her fifth birthday. It lay in great heaps along the sides of the hall, packed almost to the roofline as insulation against the wind and cold. Client warriors had cleared the pathways of Finnsburgh, and similar mounds of snow surrounded most of the cambrai and outbuildings. Gardens were still buried, and the Frisian women would plant their grains late this year.

We won't be here for that, Hildeburh told herself. We sail tonight. But she had planned her going for so long and in so many ways that she no longer truly believed she would leave. Hengest and Bjorn hoped Finn would announce the departure of the fleet for the new moon—that would give them five days to sail to Denmark, unload, and return. Their two boats, Hengest commanding the dragon-prowed ship, Bjorn the walrus, lay on the harbor beach, close to the waterline, packed with the supplies and Hildeburh's loom. The lambs were in crates, the four ponies tied amidships in Hengest's boat. They were ready.

Hildeburh missed Wealh most keenly at these times in the hall. In better years, Wealh would run to the kitchens with her mistress' final orders before the feast that they had planned together, and the banquet was always a tribute to Finn's honor, generosity, and hospitality. Now she had no part in the feast-planning. Finn had appointed a steward like the Roman kings of the old stories, and Guthlac managed Finn's storehouses and kitchens just as Freawaru had done for Hoc long ago.

There is at least one queenly duty that Guthlac cannot fulfill, she thought as she nodded to him where he stood beside the throne. The enormous chalice stood ready on a side table; only she could pass the cup and welcome the warriors—most of whom had been there since the previous fall—to Finnsburgh.

The cheers told her that Finn had entered through the king's chamber. The slaves told stories about building the new treasure-hall under the king's chamber two winters before so that Finn now slept above a wood-beamed earthen room full of gold and jewels and weapons. The treasure had been crowding out his bed and his shrine to Woden All-Father, he had said, and she could imagine him laughing loudly, his head thrown back, saying over and over that he could solve this very good problem of having too much treasure.

He walked toward his throne, easy in his kingship and authority. Raefn's death had aged him dramatically, but his legs were still firm and large, his back still straight and strong. His golden circlet studded with onyx and amethysts and pearls gleamed on his brow. The flecks of grey in his full red brown hair lent him majesty. He nodded at her without actually looking at her.

He lied to me, fourteen summers ago, she thought bitterly. He said he wanted our marriage to be more than a peace alliance. But he wants no part of comradeship or counsel. He wants sons and haemod and comfort and flattery. Well, Cynna can give him that.

She raised the cup, and a hush fell over the hall. "Welcome, allies and clients of Finn, King of the Northern and Western Seas. You gather here in noble Finnsburgh, where peace and plenty reign, before setting out to let the world know of Finn's greatness in your viking journey. Wealth and fame, husband and warriors. Hwaet!" In her heart, she toasted the last time she would have to glorify her husband before his minions. Finn took the cup, sipped the mead, and returned it to her. She bore it to the seven client kings, Hengest last as the leader of the smallest group. He spoke to her quietly through the growing din of the feast.

"I salute you, my Queen, as I drink to new life for Denmark." She smiled, glad and excited for the first time in months. Tonight we leave, she told herself again.

Higd waited in the cambrai, her own small bag packed with a little girl's treasures. Her spindle, her homespun doll, her cup, and her magic stone were her responsibility for the voyage. Hildeburh hoped her daughter was sleeping.

She handed the chalice to Guthlac and resigned herself to watch quietly from the background until Finn issued boarding orders. She sat down among the Danes, who quickly made room for her on their bench. The men had gone to Woden's Island in the harbor that day and sacrificed to their god together. Recollection of the long-ago day she had spied on the spring rituals of Odin no longer made her sick, but Hildeburh's anger had not abated over the years.

She and Bjorn had carefully, gingerly, talked about that day. The driving snow obscured the windows and made them feel splendidly isolated from the turmoil of Finnsburgh and the plight of the Danes. They spoke in the Danish of their childhood, and Higd, who didn't fully understand the language, ignored them as she worked a basic pattern on the loom.

"I never understood, princess, why the All-Father did not strike you down then and there. Perhaps Freyja interceded for you, and his wife's pleading led Odin to mercy for you," Bjorn mused as he sipped the tea she had made for him.

"Don't you think it strange that the Frisians do not believe that Odin has a wife, Bjorn?" she asked in response.

"The mysteries of Odin are different everywhere, but are all ultimately the same. Caedmon taught me much of his craft before he died, and I know the songs of power and the magic and wisdom of the battle-god.

"But I am always troubled, Hildeburh, by the famine of the Danes, and how it is that Odin allows his wife to curse our tribe. We kept his rites as best we could, and still our warriors fell, and our treasures were lost; the grain failed and the babies died." He stared into the fire. "Freyja's power over Odin is a mystery."

He doesn't look too troubled right now, she thought. Bjorn and Hengest and the other Danes seemed almost gleeful at the thought of departure. They had gone to the sacrifice that morning just like all the others.

Shouts and the sound of blows echoed briefly at the bottom of the hall. Minor arguments frequently erupted among the warriors bound together in the straitened confines of the hall; just as quickly as they started, the war band leaders broke up the quarrels. Finn rarely turned his head anymore; Hildeburh still cringed.

Finally the roasted boar was served; it had taken the hunting band nearly three days to track, kill, and butcher it. The Frisian warriors believed that by eating the boar, they ingested his spirit—his ferocity and tenaciousness. The other client warbands followed suit, and they fell upon the platters.

Finn ate the succulent leg meat, then threw the bone on the floor as he rose. "Warriors," he cried to the suddenly silent hall, "the time to journey is here!" The men cheered. "After a long winter of snow and song, we are ready to do the work of Woden All-Father. I plan to extend my dominion beyond the Ifssel Meer to the river called Rhinish by its villagers. We will sail and take tribute, make war and take plunder, and gather more allies to let the peoples of the southward know the strength of Finn and his fleet!"

The troop cheered wildly. Finn had planned the summer's voyage meticulously over the winter, consulting the client kings and his Frisian thanes, but this was the first the troops had heard of the plan. Sailing with Finn made a man rich; there was always enough plunder and tribute so that each warrior got something substantial. *They don't care where they're going or what pain they inflict,* Hildeburh thought grimly. *They just want more treasure and more songs about themselves for their bards to sing in the wintertime.*

Finn was issuing boarding orders, so she had to listen carefully. He could easily remember the array he had decided for the fleet, how many ships each client group had, which tribes worked well close together and which had to be kept apart. As he rattled off assignments, he ordered the Danes to the left rear, where there was not much glory but not much danger either. A good place for us, Hildeburh thought dully.

Finn concluded boarding orders by restating that each boat had to arrange for its own provision. And then, finally, what the whole company wanted to hear: "We leave tomorrow morning when the sun comes higher than Woden's Island."

Tomorrow? They wouldn't be able to go to Denmark. Hildeburh couldn't speak. The tightness in her chest made her feel like she wasn't breathing. Her vision clouded, then cleared. He had done it again. He had not forgotten that a Dane had killed his son, and he had had an entire winter to brood upon revenge as those very Danes unwillingly took his hospitality. The deaths of Hnaef and Raefn were meaningless. He had abandoned the peace again for a carefully contrived vengeance.

Before she could even move, Bjorn had leapt upon one of the trestle tables, banging the tip of his sheathed sword on the thick wood to order silence.

"Finn, King of the Northern and Western Seas, I bid you remember your obligations to your clients who sail with you and support you in our feats of conquest, even from the left rear, from which place the Danes beat back a Geatish ambush last summer.

"Your allies the Danes must return to Denmark before the summer voyage. Our share of last year's plunder was not jeweled circlets and golden arm-rings, as all here know well, but seed corn and turnips, lambs and livestock to overcome the famine and death that wrack our people. We could not return to our homeland in the autumn; we must return now or our homeland will wither and die like wheat in a drought.

"Allow us, Finn of Finnsburgh, four days to sail swiftly in our ships along the road of the whales to Scyldingland, where the wise grey-haired Queen Freawaru keeps our people even in their misery. Before the sun sets four times from the time of my speaking here in your great deer-antlered hall, the Danes will have joined you in good faith on your journey to Ifssel Meer. What say you, King?"

Finn leaned back in his throne, stroking the eagles carved into the wooden arms. His eyes narrowed as he stared at Bjorn, not trying to hide his hatred and contempt. Suddenly, Bjorn looked like a ragged bard with a too-elaborate sword, somewhat ridiculous standing on the trestle where moments before he had seemed glorious and electrifying. Finn did not even bother to rise for his reply.

"Boarding orders have been issued," he said narrowly, "and any allies who do not follow those orders will be considered enemies and targets for feud." He looked inquiringly around the hall. "Is that clear?"

"It is clear, my King," said Aescher firmly from the side of the throne, and beneath the babble of the hall, Hildeburh heard other mutterings of discontent. It sounded like other warriors had also wanted to see their kin after the long winter trapped in Frisia.

"Finn does not know the mercy of the White Christ," Hengest said quietly beside her. "To think of other's desires is not in him. He wants only to slaughter the Danish warriors and let the women and children die slow lonely deaths from famine. He relishes the thought. And then he will kill you, Queen, and probably your daughter too, and replace you with the red-haired woman who weaves his tunics."

"Freyja guides me now, Hengest, as your god guides you. I decided long ago that my life and my daughter's were in her hands, and I no longer agonize whether my husband will kill me now or I will continue to do her work here or in Denmark. I have visions, again, after having none for years, and I know she steers my life much as you steer your dragon-prowed ship that was my father's and then my brother's."

Bjorn threw himself onto the bench at her other side. "We're as good as dead, all of us. He just plays with us. He should have killed us last summer and gotten it over with.

"Sometimes I hate the despair of famine and weakness in our lives, and then I long to go to Valhalla and see my father, Hunlaf, and tell him of my destiny at the feast where songs are sweeter than mine and the food and drink more glorious than here in the hall of a raging king demanding vengeance and breaking the alliance. Caedmon used to say that my white-yellow hair destined me for a life of great glory or great tragedy, and I fear it has been the latter. Hengest of the White Christ and I have tried to keep alive the glories of the Danes, but there is nothing for us now."

Hildeburh and the other Danes listened quietly in the vast noise of the hall to Bjorn as he chanted what they all knew to be their death song. Finn would kill them all, and no bards would sing their praises after they were gone.

"Stately Hildeburh provided us counsel," he continued, "but even she could not know the evil of her husband's spirit as he planned to crush our people in the late coming spring when snow still clung to the shadowed side of the hall. We Danes are valiant, young and strong and noble, fighting with empty stomachs and famine-thinned arms against the enemies of Finn.

"To no avail, for he plots against us, and his allies span the seas and fill the hall, while we are but two ships. But we will die gloriously, defending our own honor and the honor of our fallen king, and we will meet in Valhalla, where the shield maidens are as beautiful and wise as our good Queen Hildeburh, daughter of Hoc and sister to Hnaef, who heals wounds with magic and sustains the Danish warband with her counsel.

"Then we will wear bright byrnies and fine arm rings, for our glory is in our loyalty to our king, and we will be richly rewarded. We will see our fathers and perhaps even our sons who died in the famine before they had grown to manhood."

"No!" raged Hengest, suddenly rising from his silence, knocking over one of the trestles. "Not my sons! Not my little boys! I cannot bear to think again of their deaths and their mother's grief! I must see Sunya again. I will forfeit a viking's glory to lay eyes upon my beloved wife once more.

We must return to our homeland and our people, for glory in the hall and the fleet of a vengeful warlord is worthless."

Hildeburh stood and surveyed the company. Finn was laughing with Cynna and his lieutenants on the dais. Some of the warbands had already headed to the ships to finish loading. Quarrels and shouts echoed among the rafters as the client kings commanded their retainers to make ready for the morning's departure. No one paid any attention to the Danes.

Guthlaf and Oslaf, two of the younger Danes, watched her fearfully. She had delivered both of the brothers early in her training, and the twins had been inseparable since they had been bundled together as newborns. She spoke, looking at them.

"What say you, young Danish warriors? Do you sail with Finn and let our people die? Or do you return to Scyldingland to have him hunt you and kill you later in the summer when the first hope of new grain springs from the Danish fields? What would Hoc or Hnaef do in this hall of treachery? How do you serve your queen now?"

The brothers rose and conferred with Hengest, who fingered his swordhilt as he nodded. Guthlaf removed a short sword from within the leather bound around his ankles. He handed it to Hengest, who concealed it in his cloak.

Guthlaf and Oslaf approached the throne. The group on the dais turned in annoyance to look at them, two ragged young men come to bother the king and his councilors.

"Finn, King of the Northern and Western seas, we Danish brothers wish to inform you of our readiness to depart in your fleet tomorrow and of our desire, should you allow it, to remain with the fleet and at Finnsburgh for the rest of our days, for Woden's strength is in you, King, and we wish to be your men."

They couldn't betray their people, Hildeburh thought as she stepped forward, about to protest. Then Bjorn caught her roughly by the arm and whispered fiercely in her ear, "Get out of here. Now. Get Higd and run for the ships. We'll join you there if we can."

In an instant, Hildeburh saw Hengest in the shadows behind Finn's throne, the dagger in his sleeve, and knew that Guthlaf and Oslaf were distracting Finn so Hengest could kill him. Trying not to run, she walked hurriedly to the side door and slipped out, then broke into a run. She ignored the cold light rain that had started to fall. As she entered her cambrai, looking frantically for her daughter, shouts erupted from the hall; a woman screamed, and Hildeburh knew it was Cynna, drenched in the blood of her master as Hengest slit Finn's throat.

In the dim firelight she saw Higd on the featherbed, the strap of her pack still slung across her torso. Hildeburh clutched Higd against her and burst back through the door as she ran toward the harbor. She skirted around the hall and raced through the unattended gate. The warrior appointed by Edgheard to guard the gate that night must have gone to the hall when the tumult started. The rain fell faster, pelting her exposed head and arms, chilling her body and stiffening her grip upon her child. Water trickled down her back from her still-short braid.

The sounds of fighting grew fainter and the sound of her own breathing louder as she rasped out air and stumbled along the rocks of the path. Higd's whimpers seemed loud as well, and through her gasping, Hildeburh reassured her as best she could. "Mama has you, sweetheart. Mama is carrying you. Mama is right here with you. Mama is here." Ahead of her she could hardly see the fleet in array on the harbor beach, the curved prows of the ships rising into the black night like the monsters of Caedmon's songs from her childhood. Some of the clients were still calmly loading their ships; the news of the battle raging in the hall had not come to the beach yet.

She heard footsteps running behind her, and turned in terror, instinctively sheltering Higd's face with her spread-wide hands. She saw Elene, a bag slung across her back, running down the path.

"Elene—get back to your mother's cambrai! This is no place for you. There is danger here."

"Queen, I'm coming with you. You know I cannot watch you leave and grow up here with no wise woman to teach me more of the goddess. You taught me to love and revere her," Elene said defiantly, "and so I love and revere you. And you're not leaving without me."

Hildeburh knew that it was pointless to waste time arguing with Elene on the beach by the boats. "Promise me," she said sternly, "that if it looks like we will not get away, you will abandon us to our fate and save yourself."

Elene didn't answer. "Let's get our ships in the water," she said and threw her bag into the boat with the walrus prow.

Bjorn and Hengest had prepared for a quick departure, though not an escape, and it was relatively easy for Elene and Hildeburh, with some help from Higd, to slide the ships over the logs into the water. The rain helped them, slickening the smooth wood of the keels and the rollers. They steadied the boats in the shallows; the keels gently grazed the bottoms. The icy water numbed their feet, and Higd did not protest when Hildeburh lifted her into the dragon-prowed ship.

Suddenly, she remembered her father's special treasure-space by the rudder and guided Higd through the benches and oars to the stern, where the trapdoor was stuck shut from long disuse. Hildeburh heaved on the heavy iron ring, which bit into her wet, chilled palm, to reveal a space just large enough for Higd to hide.

"Huddle down in there," she instructed. "I'll prop the door open so you can breathe, but don't stand up. There may be fighting. That's it. Be brave. I'll be right here. Freyja is watching over us."

Shouts and crashes echoed from the hall, and Hildeburh could see movement on the harbor path. She stood knee-deep in the harbor next to the dragon of her father and felt the seaweed stroke her legs in the rise and fall of the bay, getting rougher as the storm increased. Thunder rumbled, far off to sea, and she saw Bjorn leading the pack of Danes. Hengest brought up the rear. She saw Handschue and other warriors in pursuit. Their swords gleamed and glinted even in the darkness of very early morning, and the Danes left the path and broke into a run over the rocks and sand towards the ships.

Hildeburh stretched her arms above her head and lifted her face to the dim sky. Rain fell on her lips and cheeks and flowed into her ears and eyes. "Mother Freyja," she implored, "end this curse and save my people. Take me now, and let them go."

Her voice seemed to fill the harbor, and her chant resonated from the rocks and cliff walls, coming from her mouth although she heard the words as if another spoke them:

> *Erce, Erce, Erce, eorthan modor,*
> *AEcera wexendra and wridendra*
> *eacniendra and alniendra,*

sceafta hehra, scirra waestma,
and thaera bradan berewaetma
and thaera hwitan hwaete waestma
and ealra eeorthan waestma
Hal wes thu, folde, fira modor!

Hengest saw her in the water and shouted to the Scyldings that the ships were already launched. As they ran towards Hildeburh in the bay, a thunderous crash deafened them all, and two bolts of lightning illuminated the sky for an instant of absolute clarity. Hildeburh could see the terror and despair of her countrymen as they struggled toward her, the rage and hate on the face of Handschue, and the shock of the warriors on the beach who still had no idea what was happening.

She saw, for an instant, the odd look of surprise on Handschue's face as one of the bolts of lightning struck the golden boar on his helmet and electrified his entire body. Then her vision went dark, and she saw only sparks of light dance in the blackness as the lightning passed overhead.

The other bolt had struck an eagle-prowed ship, which burned and smoked at the center of the beach. "Come!" she cried urgently, and, as if she had woken them up, the Danes began to race towards her again.

As they reached the water, she and Elene pulled themselves into the ships. "Ready, places, go," yelled Bjorn, and the warriors seized the gunwales of the ships and began running into deeper water. "Launch," he boomed, and they leapt into the boats to their places at the benches. At the call, "oars out—and—stroke," each of the ships began to move smoothly out of the choppy harbor, four rowers on a side. The ships cut the waves directly, and she noticed that while Hengest steered and captained, Bjorn rowed as well, adjusting the rudder with his right foot as he rowed on the back left bench of the walrus-prowed ship that had been his father's.

She looked back over Hengest's shoulder towards the coastline, where it seemed that the fire was spreading. A shout echoed across the water. "The witch has killed Handschue with fire from the sky." She could see warbands drag boats to the water to keep them from flaming, but she saw no one preparing to pursue them. Then the clouds and fog and dark closed in, and she saw nothing but iron grey water.

"I don't think they're following us," she said softly, as a dim light began to grow in the eastern sky.

"No, they won't, at least not for a while," Hengest said heavily. "It seems that the Frisians are not as strong without Finn, and other allies wanted to go home too. The Eiders began cutting down Jutes as we left the hall, and other feuds erupted as well. The fleet is burned, at least in part, and without Finn, the alliance is broken, and the kings go their separate ways, no longer clients but high kings once more, and the Frisians must find a new leader—probably Aescher, since it seems that Handschue is dead as well." He looked at her curiously, but she did not respond.

"I killed your husband, my Lady. I slit his throat as he sat on his throne, and then I drew my sword and fought with his retainers who had surrounded him. They drove me half the length of the hall, and the Danes regrouped as a warband before the door of the king's chamber. Guthlaf and Oslaf provided cover as Bjorn forced the door, and we made our escape that way, through the door the red-haired whore uses. Along the way we each picked up a few things." Hengest reached into the pouch at his waist and removed Finn's circlet. "I took this from his head as the life ran from his throat. I pierced his throat the way Hnaef's was pierced, and I took his crown for the honor of my dead king. But the other Danes have treasure from Finn's chamber. With these supplies and that treasure, Lady, the Danes will live again."

Hildeburh said nothing. She leaned over and fully opened the door of Hoc's hideaway. "My treasure is enough," she said softly. She reached in and lifted Higd into her lap. The little girl's body was bluish with cold, but her wide eyes were open and alert. Hildeburh leaned against one of the benches and wrapped her sodden body around her daughter's, warming them both in an embrace. She breathed in the scent of Higd's wet hair and clutched her more tightly. In the lightening gloom of a rainy morning, she whispered to Higd until the little girl fell asleep, "You are safe, my daughter; you are safe. Mama is here, and we are safe. We are going home."

Epilogue

The nine women climbed slowly to the crest of the hill. One by one, they reached the top and stood breathing fast, nodding to each other as they scanned the ocean from the plateau.

Hildeburh saw the bay spread beneath them, the gleam of the sun on the water spangling before their eyes. Clouds hovered far off to sea, but the women stood in the light of Freyja's new risen sun. They formed a circle around the cauldron; Elene and Tecla, the other ten year old girl, lighted the fire underneath it. Hildeburh knelt before the fire and began to mix the dye.

Higd and the men—the seventeen of the war band and the one youth still alive—were inland, working the fields that had rested involuntarily during the famine. The Danes would eat berries and wild greens until the first crops came in. If they were lucky, the men would land deer or rabbits as well. Over the winter, Sunya had told Hildeburh, the seven women and one boy had huddled around the fire in the dilapidated hall, eating rations from the tiny reserve of seed corn. They had planned to trek overland and pledge themselves as slaves to the Jutes when the weather broke. Hildeburh and the warband had returned just in time.

She mixed in the dried woad, old and dusty on her fingers, and shook her head to clear her mind. The past three days had been full of emotion and action, and she was exhausted. But she knew there was much more work to do—she had a tribe to rebuild, a frithstowe to repair, fields to cultivate, and the goddess to appease.

Bjorn and Hengest had offered surprisingly little resistance when she told them they should stay in Scyldingland for the summer and help with their tribe's rebirth. She wanted Bjorn to pledge against human sacrifice at Odin's altar as well and hoped that the joy of rebuilding the tribe would show him that Freyja was stronger than Odin. He had promised to consult with his god but warned her that he still feared Freyja and Odin and their wrath.

"Hnaef's death for the honor of the Scyldings may not be enough to appease the All-Father and his wife, Lady. We have seed and lambs and willing workers, but we cannot know if the gods smile on us yet."

But Freyja is All-Mother, Hildeburh thought to herself while the cauldron boiled and its contents became a deeper blue as the woad heated into the water. *I have returned and serve her again. And I rule this tribe—all call me queen, even my mother Freawaru, and no man will take me from her again.*

She looked at her tiny mother, sitting sedately on one of the large flat boulders warmed by the rising sun. Freawaru's glory was past, her grey hair lank in a braid down her back, her skin hard and brown as leather from her frantic work in the fields as the famine descended upon her people. She wore only a homespun smock with no adornment, and Hildeburh was suddenly struck by Freawaru's resemblance to Modthryth at her death six years before. *Much has changed in those years*, she thought grimly, *yet old women are the same.*

"Sisters, daughters, mothers, we come to Freyja's hill at sunrise at a time of birth for our tribe. The goddess guides me in our ritual here today, when we do not drink the tea of birth but pledge ourselves and our children to Freyja.

"No Dane will have a child this summer. Now we make ready for the children that will come after we strengthen our land with new growth in Freyja's honor. Follow me now, and do as I do."

Freawaru stood and took Hildeburh's outstretched right hand and then gestured to Elene with her other. Sunya stood to Hildeburh's left, and soon the nine formed a ring around the fire and the cauldron with its bubbling blue contents. Hildeburh took the woad from the fire and set it on the side to cool.

The clouds were moving in from the sea, and the wind picked up. Hildeburh shivered slightly, and then put her mind back to her work. She had told the men that the women would join them in the fields before the sun was high.

"Great Mother, bless this priestess and her tribe with your fruits. Let our grains grow tall in your earth; let our sheep grow fat on your hills; let our bodies grow strong in your sun. Make us ready to bear children again in your honor. Let us worship you in the blood of birth rather than the blood of death.

"Freyja, Gefean, All-Mother, goddess of the forest groves and the inland seas and the welling rivers and the changing moon, bless our people. We few Danish women hearken to your service and paint ourselves to show our love for you."

She lifted her hands to the sky. The wind whipped her tunic about her calves and blew her short hair into her eyes. The brightness of the sun cutting through the clouds almost blinded her, but she kept her eyes open as she dropped to her knees and plunged her hands into the cauldron, full of the thickening blue liqueur.

"For Raefn, my son who died in feud. Raefn, peace in Freyja's garden," she whispered hoarsely and then smeared the dye on her face, neck, and arms.

Freawaru knelt beside her daughter, and Hildeburh could hardly hear the old woman's voice in the wind as she dipped her wrinkled hands in the woad and began to spread it on herself. "For Hnaef, my beloved son, whom my daughter saved once only for him to be killed in feud. Peace in Freyja's garden."

Salt tears mixed with the woad and ran into Hildeburh's mouth, leaving a bitter taste as she wept, again, for Raefn, and the little boy she had lost. Beside her Sunya mourned her dead sons, starved and sickened in the famine, and she suffered as she purified herself with the color of the goddess and the naming of her grief.

Rain fell as well, hard from the start, and when they had all bathed in Freyja's dye and named their dead, they joined hands and sang the song of the women's spring ritual that Bruna had taught them. They danced in a ring about the cauldron, wet with dye and tears and rain, and cried to their goddess to let them begin their lives again:

> *Freyja, ocean, mother of life,*
> *Freyja, earth, mother of all,*
> *For our daughters*
> *For our mothers*

> *Make us ripe.*
> *Freyja, air, mother of breath,*
> *Freyja, fire, warmth and then death,*
> *For your gifts*
> *For your wish*
> *Our daughters are yours.*

They stopped. They could hardly see the harbor through the sheets of rain. The fire was out.

"We will not drink together," Hildeburh cried over the now howling wind, "until we can drink to the first birth of the new Danish tribe. Let us go and work our fields and our burum and our looms so that Freyja may grace us with children next year." The other women nodded.

They bent against the wind and headed in a line for the ridge and the path. Grit blew in Hildeburh's eyes, and she squinted, trying to see the way before her. Suddenly, through the wind she heard a scream and turned around.

As she turned, a huge gust of wind roared from the south sea, and she saw enormous waves in the usually calm harbor. Tecla had lost her footing, and Elene was helping her to stand.

But as Hildeburh watched, Elene slipped too, and the wind caught her and lifted her as if she were no more than a dead leaf. The young girl's look of fear changed suddenly, to one of rapture, and through the wind Hildeburh heard

Elene cry, "The elk!" as she toppled over the cliff and into the sea.

Hildeburh screamed and fought the wind, trying to reach the edge of the headland. It was no use. The rain fell harder, and she led the remaining seven back to the frithstowe.

****

That was the beginning, child, of the New Denmark. Bruna had told me that the goddess sometimes takes a girl from the headland, and the elk had marked Elene from her birth. So the mother had her daughter with her, and the tribe grew. The men stayed home that summer and all the summers since, growing rather than fighting, though some of the young men now talk of raiding and glory again. We have babies come all year round, now, and this winter you will be old enough to help me with the easy deliveries. Tecla will have another child, I'd guess, and there will be others too. Tomorrow you will drink Freyja's tea for the first time and learn the first of her secrets.

The goddess has blessed our people, Hilda, and a princess makes a fine priestess. I will teach you her songs and her magic, her herbs and her potions. I will show you how to bring life into the world, and how to ease the leaving of it. I will teach you to trance, and you can go to her garden on your own and see your mother there, as I do. The garden of the goddess shows the priestess her own heart. I have finally learned that, after all these years.

Bjorn Hunlafing kept his promise, Hilda, and today the rites of Odin require no blood. Hengest's sons were raised to the White Christ, and I think that these two gods together show us the sides of a good man—merciful, fierce, wise, strong. Traveling bards tell us that the armies of the White Christ fight in Friesland now and show no mercy to their captives. While the Frisians have not opposed us in all my time as queen, it seems that nothing has truly changed in the land where I once was queen in name only.

No, Bjorn and I could not have married, Hilda. I could not betray the Mother again and leave her service to be Bjorn's wife. The son of Hunlaf and I meet in our spirits, and he became my companion in a way my husband never was. Your mother's death nearly killed me, and without Bjorn, I could not have borne the grief of losing Higd.

I will live, granddaughter. I will train you to rule our people and worship our goddess after I am gone. I feel the pain in my back, but no sickness grows in me as it did in your mother's breast. When you are ready, then I will go to the garden and see my mother and my daughter, and we will watch over you as you guide this land in growth and peace. Now go to sleep. I will tend the fire.

www.ingramcontent.com/pod-product-compliance
Lightning Source LLC
Chambersburg PA
CBHW060623260626
47161CB00008B/2788